Mei's jaw drop~~ed~~ I got whatever I wa~~nted, on some silver~~ platter? Or that my life here was *happy*?"

Jack hadn't meant to insult her, but from the mixture of hurt and defensiveness in her eyes, apparently he had. "Sorry."

She shifted uncomfortably. "Me, too. Coming back here has made me…oversensitive, or something," she added.

She headed out the door, and without another word, she strode down the hallway with her heels clicking against the floor in a rapid staccato beat.

He watched her go. Five more sessions in her classroom meant five more opportunities to see if he could get past Mei Clayton's prickly defenses. Did she have a warm heart hidden behind all of that armor?

Rocky Mountain Heirs:
When the greatest fortune of all is love.

The Nanny's Homecoming—Linda Goodnight
July 2011

The Sheriff's Runaway Bride—Arlene James
August 2011

The Doctor's Family—Lenora Worth
September 2011

The Cowboy's Lady—Carolyne Aarsen
October 2011

The Loner's Thanksgiving Wish—Roxanne Rustand
November 2011

The Prodigal's Christmas Reunion—Kathryn Springer
December 2011

Books by Roxanne Rustand

Love Inspired

†*Winter Reunion*
†*Second Chance Dad*
The Loner's Thanksgiving Wish

Love Inspired Suspense

Hard Evidence
Vendetta
Wildfire
Deadly Competition
**Final Exposure*
**Fatal Burn*
**End Game*
**Murder at Granite Falls*

*Snow Canyon Ranch
**Big Sky Secrets
†Aspen Creek Crossroads

ROXANNE RUSTAND

lives in the country with her husband and a menagerie of pets, many of whom find their way into her books. She works part-time as a registered dietitian at a psychiatric facility, but otherwise you'll find her writing at home in her jammies, surrounded by three dogs begging for treats, or out in the barn with the horses. Her favorite time of all is when her kids are home—though all three are now busy with college and jobs.

This is her twenty-fifth novel. *RT Book Reviews* nominated her for a Career Achievement Award in 2005, and she won the magazine's award for Best Superromance of 2006.

She loves to hear from readers! Her snail-mail address is P.O. Box 2550, Cedar Rapids, Iowa, 52406-2550. You can also contact her at: www.roxannerustand.com, www.shoutlife.com/roxannerustand or at her blog, where readers and writers talk about their pets: www.roxannerustand.blogspot.com.

The Loner's Thanksgiving Wish
ROXANNE RUSTAND

Love Inspired

Special thanks and acknowledgment to Roxanne Rustand for her participation in the Rocky Mountain Heirs miniseries.

Recycling programs
for this product may
not exist in your area.

™ LOVE INSPIRED BOOKS

ISBN-13: 978-0-373-87704-1

THE LONER'S THANKSGIVING WISH

www.LoveInspiredBooks.com

Printed in U.S.A.

"For know that I have plans for you," declares the Lord, "plans to prosper you and not harm you, plans to give you hope and a future."
—*Jeremiah* 29:11

With thanks and appreciation
to all of the wonderful authors who were
part of the Rocky Mountain Heirs series.

Chapter One

Mei Clayton veered off the trail near the summit of Belle's Peak, found the edge of the cliff where she'd often picnicked as a teenager and surveyed the panorama of rugged ranching country below.

To the west, shadowed by the massive, snowy peaks of the Rocky Mountains, lay the distant, rustic cowboy town of Clayton, Colorado. Her hometown, named after a great-grandfather she'd never met. The last place she wanted to be.

Especially for an entire, interminable year, though that's exactly what she had to do, thanks to a stipulation in her grandpa George's will.

A year—but not one day more.

Mei and each of her five cousins all had to comply, or none would receive a single penny. And though Mei would have preferred to continue teaching in San Francisco, she just couldn't let the others lose out on the inheritance some of them badly needed.

Delaying her inevitable, awkward arrival, she'd parked along the highway to hike one of the easier trails in this part of the Rockies, just to savor one of the few good memories she'd kept close to her heart during her years away.

Maybe she'd never felt accepted by the Clayton family, but she'd loved every moment that she spent hiking and climbing these rugged peaks.

Yet even up here, she hadn't found a sense of solitude and peace. The snow-dusted trail offered an easy climb and breathtaking vistas, and she'd already run into several other local hikers taking advantage of the bright sunshine on this first weekend of November.

She'd hoped to do a little climbing and had brought her gear in a backpack. But the snow was deeper at this higher elevation, and she needed to turn back. Get in her car. And face her return to the town she'd so desperately wanted to leave as a teen.

Though it was her impending conversation with her widowed mother that truly had her stomach tying itself in a tight knot. How would Mom react when she heard the news about her son? Lucas had been in a few scrapes when he was a teenager, but nothing like the one he was in now.

At the sound of voices and the merry jingle of bear bells, she stopped at one side of the trail to let a pair of hikers pass.

One of them continued on, but the girl pulled to a stop. "Mei?"

Mei looked up in surprise at the pretty teenager standing in front of her in a puffy pink down jacket and jeans. "Jasmine?"

Her cousin Arabella's ward tucked a long strand of silky brown hair behind her ear, her eyes sparkling. "What are you doing back in Colorado so soon? We didn't expect you until Christmas."

Warmed by the girl's obvious happiness, Mei felt some of her tension ease. "I…had a change of plans."

"Well, I think it's great you're here. Arabella has been

looking forward to you living in town again, and now you'll be here in time for the wedding!"

"Whose?" Mei recalled her mother's last email—a rare event in any case—that had mentioned the latest romance involving Jasmine's foster mother, and smiled. "Arabella and Dr. Turner? Already?"

A flash of confusion crossed the girl's face. "Mine. You didn't hear about it?

"*Yours?*" Mei asked faintly.

Jasmine had lived with Arabella for a couple years and had graduated from high school this past spring. Maybe she was of legal age, but…

"We're getting married on Christmas Eve." Jasmine's smile widened as her hiking partner turned back to join her. "You remember Cade, right?"

"Cade *Clayton?*" A flood of memories rushed through Mei as she stared up at the handsome young man in a denim jacket and jeans looping an arm protectively around Jasmine's shoulders.

Oh, she remembered Cade, all right. Years ago, his mother had married Mei's infamous uncle Charley.

Memories flooded back from the day when Mei was getting her hair trimmed at the Hair Today beauty salon and Cade's mother happened to be sitting in the next chair.

Lorelei freely admitted she'd picked the wrong branch of the family tree and *definitely* the wrong man.

She'd claimed the only good thing that came out of her marriage was little Cade…but she was sure glad that at least her older son Jack was no blood kin to the Claytons.

Mei had been all ears because, at the time, she'd been in the throes of a long and futile high school crush on Jack— one of the more embarrassing points in her life.

Even after ten years she felt a blush warm her cheeks. He'd been way out of her league. She'd known it from the start, but the humiliating whispers among her classmates about her foolish crush had been even more painful. Her cousin Vincent had been the worst—no surprise there. His relentless taunts had felt like jabs of a knife to her heart, and she was still sure that he'd been the one to start the cruel gossip in the first place.

Cade had just been a little guy when Mei and Jack were in high school, and she hadn't seen him since. Now built like a football player, only his tawny hair and warm brown eyes were familiar.

He gave a low, self-conscious laugh. "I guess the last time you saw me I was starting grade school."

Mei laughed. "If that."

"Weren't you in high school with my brother?"

"Um…yes."

When a few drops of sleet hit Jasmine's cheek, she batted them away with her fluffy white mittens. "Maybe we'd all better get moving. Cade and I want to make it up to the first waterfall, and then we're heading back to town."

Mei eyed the slate-gray clouds crawling over the mountain peaks. "Are you sure? Maybe you'd better start down with me."

"Nah—just a few minutes more." Jasmine patted the pocket of her light jacket. "I want to take some pictures up there. I hear it's like a wintry fairyland, with those shimmering icicles covering the trees from the spray of the falls. It might be good as a background for the cover of our wedding programs."

"*W-wedding* programs?" Mei felt her jaw drop. So the girl was really serious about this.

Jasmine's smile turned radiant. "Won't it be pretty?"

Mei belatedly remembered to snap her mouth shut. "It… it certainly will."

What were these two thinking? And why hadn't the adults in their lives tried to steer them away from such a huge commitment right out of high school?

Cade grinned, obviously reading her expression. "We got the same reaction from everyone else at first, too. But we're certain, and we're ready. And we're already planning to go on to college, believe me."

"We have to hurry off right now," Jasmine added apologetically. "But maybe you can come over to Arabella's sometime to hear all the details."

"I'll do that, I promise." Mei managed a weak wave as the two of them started back on the path.

What they decided to do was hardly her business, after all. Neither of them were a relative of hers. *And it's not like my own choices brought me happiness, either,* she thought as she took a deep breath and surveyed her surroundings.

Even with the darkening clouds, it was a perfect day. And how could it not be when she was surrounded by God's perfect glory in every towering mountain peak, in every call of a Pine Grosbeak and its mate from the top of the Engelmann spruce towering overhead?

Quiet joy started to bubble up inside her as she made her way down the path. Adopted from China as a baby, she'd always felt like an outsider in both her extended family and this small ranching community where no one else looked like her. With a stern father and a cool, distant mother, there hadn't been much warmth and connection with her immediate family, either, except with her younger brother, Lucas.

But she'd been gone a long time. She was grown up now; stronger and more mature. And she now realized that she was as much at fault as anyone if she hadn't been well accepted as a child. Painfully shy and withdrawn, maybe she'd seemed standoffish.

Perhaps this move back home wouldn't be so bad, after all. Maybe it would even bring an opportunity for her to truly connect with her mother and extended family, and finally feel accepted as one of the Claytons—something she'd longed for all her life.

Mei was startled out of her daydream by a bloodcurdling scream that tore through the air, followed by the deafening sound of boulders crashing down a slope. The crack of trees splintering. And then a deathly silence fell.

Jasmine?

Mei spun on her heel, terror grabbing her by the throat as she raced in the direction of the scream and pulled to a stunned halt.

A few dozen yards up the trail, a raw, gaping crater at least ten feet across had been gouged out of the edge of a cliff where there'd been a trail just minutes before. Cade and Jasmine were nowhere to be seen. Had they dashed past the crumbling ground in time?

She grabbed a sturdy pine branch and looked over the edge. *Please, Lord, let them both be safe.* "Jasmine! Cade!"

No one answered.

There was barely a haze of snow on the floor of the ravine below, and a cloud of dust still boiled upward, obliterating the view of the bottom.

Wherever it was.

"Wow," a woman exclaimed. "If we'd come down the trail a few seconds earlier we would've been caught in that landslide."

Her heart hammering against her ribs, Mei tore her gaze from the bottom of the ravine and stared at the two women who had materialized on the other side of the trail.

Mei closed her eyes for a brief moment and said another silent prayer. "There were two hikers here a minute ago—a teenage girl and her boyfriend. Did they pass you?"

The women exchanged glances, then shook their heads, their eyes widening with horror as they moved closer to the edge.

Mei waved them back. "The rest of this area could be unstable. Stay over by those trees."

The taller woman paled. "It sounded like thunder when the cliff gave way."

A wave of dread curled through Mei as she scanned the bottom of the ravine.

Falling boulders had carved deep, raw gouges in the steep walls of the ravine. Even now, smaller rocks were shifting and falling. From somewhere far below came the sound of pebbles skittering down the cliff.

A massive boulder big as a car broke free, vibrating the ground beneath her feet as it bounced down the rocky wall and catapulted in slow motion out into the dust-filled emptiness. The distant explosion of shattering rock at the bottom shook the earth.

"Cade! Jasmine!" Mei shouted their names over and over, straining to hear a response. *Please, God, let them be safe. They're just so young.*

They could well have been in the path of that last boulder, though if they'd survived their fall, it would be amazing.

Jerking off her backpack, Mei checked the reception bars on her cell phone. No Service flashed on the screen, dashing her hopes. There was no time to run for help. She needed to get to the bottom of that ravine without delay.

She looked up at the ghost-white faces of the other two women. "There's an emergency phone in the shelter at the base of the trail. Tell the ranger to call for help. We need a rescue team with climbing gear—be sure to tell them that. And we'll need an ambulance, too."

The two hikers stood frozen for a split second, staring at the place where there'd once been a trail.

"Go!"

Jarred into action, they gave the rockslide wide berth and raced away down the trail.

Mei dumped the contents of her backpack on the ground. First aid kit. High-energy bars. Several water bottles. Leather gloves. The bright orange coils of her favorite old Mammut climbing rope and a handful of carabiners in a Ziploc bag.

She'd done a lot of climbing up here as a teenager, and she'd continued the sport in the mountain ranges in the Southwest. Her climbing gear had been the first thing she'd packed for her move back to Colorado.

Now, she looked heavenward and murmured a quiet "thanks" for the impulse to stop and hike this particular trail on her way home.

But was her rope even long enough?

She didn't have enough length to rappel down with a belay device to control her descent, so it would have to be a far more dangerous drop—hand over hand down a single length of rope anchored near the top of the cliff.

Swirls of dust still eddied at the bottom of the ravine. Where were Cade and Jasmine…beneath that boulder, or under the landslide that had sucked them off the trail?

She tied one end of her rope to a stout pine trunk and threw the coils over the edge, then shouldered her backpack. From somewhere far below came a faint cry for help.

Mei's heart leaped with joy. At least one of them was alive and conscious—and that meant there was hope for both. *Thank you, God!*

She donned her leather gloves, then lowered herself

over the edge and started down. Another faint cry for help echoed through the ravine.

"I'm coming," Mei shouted. Her heart pounding against her ribs, she slowly lowered herself hand over hand. "Hang on."

"Mei—over here," Jasmine yelled. "Hurry. C-Cade's hurt."

And there she was, on a long, narrow ledge hidden from view from the cliff above by a clump of vegetation.

At the last five feet of her rope, Mei clung to the rough, rocky wall and sparse vegetation to descend the final fifteen or twenty feet.

"I'm so glad you're here with me," Jasmine cried.

"And I'm glad to be here." The teenager was scraped and battered from her fall, with deep red bruises that would turn black by tomorrow. But she was alert and coherent, *praise the Lord.* Her face white as chalk, she held Cade's head cradled in her lap, holding a blood-soaked athletic sock against his temple. He wasn't moving. "Has Cade been awake at all?"

"N-no." Tears spilled down Jasmine's grimy cheeks as she watched Mei shrug off her backpack and pull out an emergency first aid kit. "I was afraid nobody would c-come. A-and it would g-get dark, and c-cold, and Cade w-wouldn't have a chance."

"Take a slow, deep breath, honey. I've already sent for help. A rescue team is going to get both of you out of here in no time."

Any rescue attempt wasn't going to be easy, though. It was more than a hundred feet to the top, with no trails in sight for a rescue team with a stretcher. The ravine was too deep and narrow, with multiple overhanging ledges, to bring in a helicopter.

Even if a copter dropped a basket, the slightest wind

up top could send the litter swinging wildly against the narrow vertical rock walls on either side.

The best chance would be to hike out following the creek bed—if it led to easier access within a reasonable distance and not a dead end.

Mei closed her eyes briefly, bringing her last CPR and first aid training session into sharp focus. She knelt at the boy's side and timed his erratic respirations. She checked his pulse—weak but steady.

"He's breathing," Jasmine whispered brokenly. "I keep feeling for his pulse. He fell *so* hard. H-he was trying to save me from falling when the ground buckled. I got caught in some bushes that slowed my fall, but C-Cade..."

Mei eyed the sock pressed against the boy's temple, then searched through her first aid kit for a roll of bandaging. "Smart thinking, Jasmine. I don't want to risk disturbing the clotting of that wound, so we'll leave that cloth there and overwrap it with this gauze to keep the pressure steady."

She looked up and gave the girl an encouraging smile as she wound the bandage around Cade's head several times and pressed the end of the bandage in place. "This material sticks to itself, so it should hold well. But I'm going to ask you to sit still and not jostle his head, okay?"

"I'm scared, Mei." Jasmine's voice quavered.

"Head wounds always bleed a lot, so he might be just fine otherwise. But he could have a bad concussion, and if he has got any spinal injuries we don't want to take a chance."

Jasmine nodded, her lower lip trembling and her eyes filling with fear. "M-maybe I hurt him already, just trying to make him comfortable."

Maybe, but it was done. And trying to keep Cade stable

while managing a hysterical girl wouldn't do either of them any good.

"You've done your best—and if you hadn't thought so fast, he could've lost a lot more blood."

Mei began a careful head-to-toe exam, gently palpating the unconscious boy for obvious fractures and searching for other wounds. The ugly dark bruising and swelling of his right ankle didn't look good. His jacket and sweatshirt were torn, revealing multiple lacerations and bruising on his ribs and shoulders.

Using sterile four-by-four gauze squares and the roll of bandaging material, Mei wrapped his wounds.

Jasmine kept her gaze fixed on his face. "I love you so much, Cade," she choked out. "You have to be okay because you and I are going to grow old together. You can't leave me now. You just can't."

Mei lifted his eyelids, checking for even pupil reactions. Was the right one more sluggish? Hard to tell, in these shadows, and she wished she had a flashlight. But if the pupils were uneven, what could she do? The first aid kit was the extent of what she had to work with.

And what worried her the most was his lack of responsiveness. A head injury could easily be fatal. Even now, his brain could be swelling.

And his spine…

Mei said a long, silent prayer as the minutes ticked by, then kept up a steady patter of small talk to distract Jasmine.

A half hour passed.

Then another.

Blood still seeped through the makeshift bandages. Noticing it was worse at Cade's temple, Mei added another layer of bandaging, then applied gentle pressure.

Shouts of excitement erupted from the top of the cliff.

"They're almost here!" a woman shouted. "Three county rescue guys!"

Jasmine closed her eyes and sighed with obvious relief. "Thank you, God. I've been praying this whole time for help to get here." Her gaze shot up the sides of the ravine. "But how—what can they do?"

"This is their job, honey," Mei said with more confidence than she felt. "They do this sort of thing all the time."

In minutes, one man in sunglasses, a dark jacket and a COUNTY SEARCH & RESCUE–emblazoned backpack quickly rappelled down into the ravine, while the other two rescuers stayed at the top and watched, presumably awaiting directions.

Relief and gratitude welled up in Mei's chest until she was barely able to speak. "Thank you, thank you," she finally managed, fighting back the sting of tears in her eyes as the first man reached them. "I'm so glad—"

Her next words froze in her throat when she realized just who he was…and, with the next heartbeat, recognized the tragic irony of him being the first one on the scene.

Although he was all too familiar to Mei now that he'd removed his shades and black ball cap, he didn't even glance her way because his attention was riveted on Cade.

He was all business, pure professional skill, as he hunkered down next to the injured boy. Working rapidly, he opened up his duffel bag and withdrew a stethoscope and portable blood pressure cuff, donned vinyl gloves, then began a careful exam.

But she'd seen his split second of hesitation.

The shock in his eyes.

And the way he'd blanched before throwing himself

into EMT mode. Of all the people in the world to answer this call, Jack McCord had shown up.

And Cade was his half brother.

Chapter Two

From the moment he reached the ledge, Jack riveted his attention on the still form of his brother.

Jasmine looked up at him. "I c-can't believe you're here," she whispered, her voice laced with panic. "Can you help him? *Please*—"

"Just hold his head steady. Don't move. And be quiet, honey."

Shoving aside his own whirlwind of emotions, Jack pulled on his vinyl gloves and forced himself into professional mode. He swiftly checked Cade's vitals, relaying the data to the emergency room staff at the small local hospital through the cell phone headset on his ear.

Breathing—shallow but steady.

Pulse—regular.

Blood pressure—a hundred over sixty-eight.

Skin—cool and dry.

Pupils—uneven, the right more sluggish than the left. Unresponsive.

Slight signs of shock, with a possibility of internal injuries and a head injury.

But thank you, Lord. Cade appears stable.

Jack quickly checked him for bleeding and found he'd

already been capably bandaged, then he searched for obvious fractures. Finally, rocking back on his heels, he listened to the E.R. doctor, disconnected and called his team members waiting at the top of the cliff.

He pulled a reflective foil blanket from his backpack and tucked it around Cade, then gently rested his hand against his brother's cheek. "Cade—can you hear me?"

No response.

A heavy fist clamped down on Jack's heart as his thoughts raced through a litany of fears for his only brother. Internal injuries could be hemorrhaging unseen. He could have sustained a serious brain injury or damage to the spinal cord. He'd fallen more than an hour ago. If he wasn't responding right now, what were the chances of an extended coma…or death? *Lord, please take care of him. Please keep him safe in Your hands—let his injuries be minor, and please, please help him heal.*

"How is he, Jack?" Jasmine's voice shook. "I'm so scared for him."

Whatever his own fears, inciting panic at this point wouldn't do anyone any good. He considered his answer carefully. "I don't see any significant external wounds. At least, he isn't bleeding through any of the bandages so far. And I haven't found obvious fractures. Of course, Cade isn't awake to tell us where he hurts most, and I'm not a doctor. I also don't have a radiologist's X-ray report in front of me. We'll have answers soon, though."

Desperate hope flared to life in Jasmine's eyes. "So that's good?"

"Yes, it is. And his heartbeat, color and breathing are surprisingly steady given what he's just been through." Trying to stay positive in light of the very serious possibilities made it hard to meet her earnest gaze.

"Then why doesn't he wake up?" Tears trickled down her dirt-smudged cheeks.

"Maybe he just has a concussion and will be coming around soon."

"What if it isn't that? What if…" Her voice trailed off.

Jack sighed heavily and glanced toward the other woman, who had stepped away when he arrived and now stood at the far edge of the ledge with her head bowed, her long black hair veiling the side of her face. "I don't have the answers. But we'll have him out of here in no time, and the E.R. will be ready for him. They'll figure everything out."

She sniffled and backhanded the tears from her face. "I just can't believe this happened, and it's all my fault. If I had agreed to go back to the car instead of insisting on going up the trail…"

"But it isn't your fault. A terrible coincidence, maybe, being at the wrong place at that very moment. But you couldn't have predicted it would happen." He studied her closely. "What about you? Looks like you need to be checked over, too."

She lifted a cautious hand to her face. "Just a few bumps and scrapes. Maybe a little sprain of my wrist. It's Cade who needs your attention. Not me."

"You'll still need to be seen in the E.R." Her color had improved and she appeared to be calmer since he'd first arrived. He moved next to her, noting that her skin was warm and dry as he took her pulse and blood pressure. Both normal.

He gently bandaged a laceration on her arm, then examined her swollen wrist and wrapped it with a splint and a firm, supportive bandage.

"I'd guess that the doctor will want an X-ray of your wrist at the very least, and you might need some sutures."

He slowly straightened and pulled off his gloves, then donned a clean pair as he returned to Cade and knelt at his side. He looked over his shoulder at the other woman. "And what about you, ma'am?"

She still stood facing away from him, her arms wrapped around her slender waist, but now she turned slowly toward him with a tentative expression. "Hi, Jack."

He felt his jaw drop and his heart lurch against his ribs. If he'd discovered the Queen of England standing in front of him, he couldn't have been more surprised. Just seeing her slammed him back to his tongue-tied teenage years. "*Mei?* What on earth…"

Mei Clayton had always been pretty. Her delicate features and dark eyes had made her seem as exotic and untouchable as one of his mother's porcelain figurines. But now, ten years after high school, she was no longer just pretty—she was *beautiful*.

"I was hiking and had intended to do some climbing farther up the mountain." She dropped her gaze to Cade's still form. "I'm so glad I was close by with my climbing gear. When Jasmine and Cade fell, I did what I could."

He'd seen her rope dangling down the face of the cliff, and didn't even want to imagine such a fragile woman making that dangerous descent—especially because it was at least ten feet too short. One false move and she might have fallen to her death. "You are one brave woman. And you did a fine job with the first aid, too."

"I just wish I'd had more rope for the trip down."

He cleared his throat, still feeling a little stunned at running into her in such an unlikely place. "I'd heard that all of you had to be home by Christmas. What brings you back home so soon?"

Her expression clouded. "My brother is missing somewhere in the Everglades. I wanted to be here with my mom while we wait for news."

"I'm sorry. I haven't seen Lucas since I left for college, but I remember that he was always a capable guy...and very independent."

"One of the reasons he and my parents didn't see eye to eye. I hear he hasn't even been back here since graduating from high school. Still, he managed to put himself through veterinary school, so I just know he's going to be a success. If..." Her voice trailed off.

"Lucas is a resourceful guy." Jack rechecked Cade's blood pressure and pulse, then examined his bandages for any seepage. "I'll bet your worries will be unfounded when he suddenly turns up one of these days."

"I sure hope so." She bit her lower lip, as if debating about saying more about her brother. "How long until Cade gets to the hospital?"

"The other two guys on the rescue team are looking for a good route for bringing him up. The EMTs and an ambulance are on the way. Maybe an hour?"

"Oh, that long," she breathed. She rested a hand on Jasmine's shoulder. "I guess we'd all better be praying then."

Jasmine nodded. "Believe me, I already have."

Jack held Cade's hand as the ambulance bounced and swayed down the rugged mountain road toward town and listened to the steady beep of a monitor mounted on the wall. "He looks stable, right?"

Sue, the EMT who had chosen to ride in back, was sitting on the bench next to Jack. She glanced up at the screen and nodded. "From what I see, I think he's doing well, all things considered. He's one very lucky boy."

"I just wish he would wake up." Jack gave his brother's

hand a squeeze. "I haven't seen him this quiet since he was a newborn—and that wasn't for a very long stretch at a time."

"I'm sure the docs at the hospital will be doing MRIs and X-rays to make sure he—" She peered at Cade's face. "I think I saw his eyelids flicker. Cade, can you hear me?"

A moment later Cade's eyelids fluttered, then opened halfway.

"You're in an ambulance. You had quite a fall, cowboy." Jack brushed a wayward lock of hair from Cade's forehead, willing him to say something. *Anything.*

When he didn't, anxiety snaked through Jack's stomach and began tying it into a tight knot.

The EMT leaned over so she could look directly into Cade's eyes. "What's your name?"

His brow furrowed, as if he were calling up a distant memory, before he finally silently moved his lips to form his name.

"Do you know where you are? What town you live in?"

He stared blankly at her.

"Do you know what day it is?"

Again, a blank look.

The EMT sat back on the bench. "The doctors will be checking him for a concussion. But it's a really good sign that he's waking up and that he's at least oriented to his name."

A good sign, maybe, but Jack longed to hear Cade's voice. To hear him crack a joke—or even renew their old argument about Cade's decision to marry so young. Anything that would show he hadn't suffered a serious head injury.

"I'm here with you and I'm not leaving," Jack reassured him. "We'll make sure the docs fix you up good as new."

But Cade didn't answer, and Jack's heart grew heavier with each passing mile.

Chapter Three

At the small community hospital, Mei sat with Jasmine in one of the exam rooms and listened to the bustle of activity several rooms away.

"We should hear something soon, honey," she murmured, holding the girl's trembling hand. "Don't worry. So far the news has all been good, right? The doc doesn't think you have any fractures or internal injuries. You'll be out of here in a little while."

During the past several hours, a nurse had been in to clean Jasmine's scrapes and take a health history. Later, a doctor with Angela Kerber, M.D., embroidered on her lab coat provided an exam and several sutures to close a laceration. Results of the X-rays and the CT of Jasmine's abdomen were due back anytime.

But Jasmine's attention had been riveted on Cade since the accident, and she'd barely paid attention to the doctor's words about her own condition.

"I don't care about me. Cade is the one who fell the hardest. When are they going to tell me about *him?*" Clad in a thin exam gown and wrapped in a white cotton blanket, Jasmine sat at the edge of her gurney and shuddered. "Maybe…they're afraid to let me know."

"But he's fully awake and talking now. So that's a great sign. And we're both praying for him, right? And I'm sure his brother is also."

Jasmine glanced at the big white clock on the wall. "Arabella left for Denver this afternoon with her girls to see Jonathan. I just wish she could be here, too."

"When will she be back?"

"N-not 'til late this evening." A tear slid down Jasmine's cheek. "Wh-what if he doesn't m-make it?"

Footsteps stopped just outside, and the curtain rustled. Jack cleared his throat. "All right if I come in?"

"Absolutely." Her gaze lowered, Mei slipped out of her chair and made room for him to reach the side of Jasmine's gurney.

Even without meeting his eyes, she was all too aware of his strong, muscular build—toned and refined and even more powerful than the boy she'd admired back in high school. He'd matured to a good six feet, with an aura of easy confidence that surrounded him. Did all of the local gals still hang on his every word, and bask in his trademark smile? That charming, sidelong grin had sure melted hearts back in high school.

She could personally attest to that.

"Thought I'd better come in and check on you two ladies," he said, his voice low and warm. He bent down a little to meet Jasmine's gaze straight on. "Cade is worried about you, so I told him I'd see how you're holding up in here. Looks to me like you're in fine shape. Any good news yet?"

Jasmine grabbed on to his arm with both hands. "I'm okay, but the nurses won't tell me *anything* about Cade, and they wont let me go to him, either. Is it bad?"

"We're still waiting for the results of his CT scans and X-rays. But so far, so good. He doesn't seem to have any fractures, anyway." He searched her face, and gently tucked a long strand of her hair behind her ear. "He cares a great deal about you, but you already know that."

"Thank you, Jack. Please tell him that I'm fine. I just wish I could get out of this room and go to him."

"I'm heading back to him right now. I'll let him know." Jack glanced over his shoulder at Mei and winked. "Keeping Jasmine here all this time must've been a challenge."

A light, witty response would've been perfect.

Or a thoughtful expression of concern.

But now, feeling as awkward as she'd been back in high school, Mei could only summon a small shrug in return, and memories assailed her as she watched Jack leave the room.

"You two have known each other a long time, haven't you?" Jasmine asked, giving Mei a curious look. "Like, did you two ever date?"

Surprised, Mei laughed. "Whatever gave you that idea?"

"He's handsome. You're pretty. You're both nice and about the same age."

Oh, the simple logic of youth—imagining that anything in the world was possible if only one wished for it. "No, we never did."

Jasmine fidgeted on the gurney. "So tell me all about things back then. When Cade's mother came to town and all."

"Haven't you and Cade talked about all of that already?"

Jasmine made a face. "His version. But guys skip all the good stuff."

"Good stuff?"

"The details." She shot yet another impatient glance at

the clock. "And the way things are going, we could be here forever."

"So you're bored and need a distraction. Okay…very well." Mei pulled a chair closer to Jasmine and sat down. "This is a small town, and it was even more quiet ten years ago. Jack was a grade ahead of me, but I still remember the day he showed up at elementary school."

"Love at first sight?" Jasmine teased.

Mei folded her arms over her chest. "Not then *or* now, young lady."

"Please—go on."

"His mother had just married my uncle Charley, and newcomers in school weren't that common in this dusty ranching town back then. But although most new kids were withdrawn at first, Jack had a chip on his shoulder from the first day I saw him walk into Ms. Berkowski's fourth-grade classroom. He made no effort to talk to anyone on the playground or anywhere else." She released a breath. "Now that I'm a teacher, I realize he was probably trying to hide the fact that he was scared. He was facing a lot of changes in his life, with a new stepfather and a new school."

Yawning, Jasmine swung her legs up onto the gurney and rested her head on the pillow. "Cade says Jack was mad about his mom's marriage. He says Jack and Charley never got along."

"I wouldn't know about that. I just know that Lorelei's marriage to Charley lasted only a few years—not much beyond Cade's birth—but she and the kids stayed on in town nonetheless."

"So did you and Jack ever get to be friends?"

Mei smiled. "Have you forgotten elementary school? Boys are a lower life-form at that age. Wrestling and yelling and being rowdy."

"What about high school?"

"Different social circles, I guess."

Jasmine levered herself up on one elbow to look at Mei. "Did you know Cade?"

"I saw him around town. He was the cutest little boy ever, with those big brown eyes."

"Then why didn't Charley try to be a good, attentive dad? He had shared custody, but Cade says he failed to show up most of the time and yelled a lot when he did have Cade with him. It's so unfair." Her expression clouded. "And it's even unfair now."

"Why is that?"

"You should *hear* the things he says about Cade and me getting married."

"About how young you both are?"

Jasmine rolled her eyes. "Everyone has brought that up. He's worse, saying crazy stuff about how I'm in cahoots with your grandpa George's 'clan' since I've been living with Arabella. And how Cade has no business getting mixed up with the likes of them. Granted, Charley's always been volatile, but these accusations are ridiculous!"

"There's some bad history between the two sides of the family," Mei said carefully.

Jasmine snorted. "*Old* history."

"Painful, to some."

"But it's all in the past. I know about how your grandpa cheated his brother in some sort of land deal that left George rich and Samuel poor, and how Samuel has been mad ever since."

It was hard coming up with a defense of anyone's actions—but Samuel's side of the family tree had found endless ways to cause trouble over the years in retaliation. "Maybe…Charley is only following his father's lead, then."

"But it shouldn't drive Cade and me apart. It just isn't fair." She sighed. "That's why I'm thinking about putting on a big Thanksgiving dinner all by myself for both sides of the family. If I can get everyone face to face, maybe they'll finally grow up."

Ah, the innocence of youth. "It might not work out *quite* that way."

"But someone needs to try," Jasmine said with a stubborn lift of her chin. "And because I have the most at stake right now, I guess it needs to be me."

"What does Cade think of all this?"

Jasmine's mouth twitched. "He doesn't think anyone will show up, but I think they will. And he knows how much this means to me."

"Just be careful to not pressure people too much, honey. I'm not saying you don't have the right idea, but there's a long, long history between some of these people, and what some of them have done to seek revenge against each other has left a lot of open wounds." She shrugged. "Maybe some battles aren't worth the cost."

"Well, this one is."

Mei arched a brow.

Jasmine yawned again and closed her eyes, and in a few minutes her breathing became deep and even. Poor thing—she had to be exhausted from all she'd been through.

Mei grabbed the only magazine in the cubicle—an old *Sports Illustrated*—and settled back in her chair with the magazine unopened in her lap. Life could sure change in a second. A dangerous landslide, the unexpected arrival of Jack McCord…

He'd been just another boy to her during elementary school, but she hadn't shared the rest of the story with Jasmine. Things certainly changed in high school, when his dark, sun-streaked blond hair and tall, muscular physique reminded her of a Californian surfer and his reckless, defiant attitude promised trouble. His bad-boy allure had been undeniable.

But beneath that tough shell of his she'd glimpsed something else that had touched her heart. A flash of pain and loneliness in those mesmerizing blue eyes, coupled with an undercurrent of simmering anger that flashed fire if anyone mentioned the name of his former stepfather.

Mei had known from the first moment of girlish attraction that, though he was far beyond the reach of a shy nobody like her, they were far more alike than anyone could've ever guessed. *Soul mates,* she'd thought then, with the naïveté of a young girl.

She'd tried to hide her secret, painful crush on him. Then she'd been humiliated beyond measure when her cousin Vincent somehow ferreted out her feelings and broadcast them throughout the school with vicious glee.

The gentle sympathy in Jack's eyes when they bumped into each other in the school library a few weeks later had made her humiliation a thousand times worse because then she'd known that he'd heard the gossip and *felt sorry* for her.

Her one saving grace had been that he'd gone off to college somewhere on the West Coast and had shaken the dust of Clayton, Colorado, off his feet long ago, while Mei had headed for college in the opposite direction the following year. She hadn't expected to ever run into him again.

Yet her traitorous heart had picked up an extra beat at just seeing him again. She'd been sure that he would've forgotten her—it would be no surprise. She'd been nearly invisible back in school, just an inconsequential shadow in a sea of boisterous students who'd excluded her.

Though if Jack *had* looked her way, there wouldn't have been any chance to date him.

She shuddered, remembering once again the vehement dislike between the two branches of the Clayton family tree. Maybe Jasmine and Cade's generation would finally bring peace to the family, but that hadn't been a glimmer of a possibility before.

Grandpa George's side was filled with good-hearted, hardworking folks, whereas his brother Samuel's side was filled with resentful ne'er-do-wells who seemed to cause endless trouble...or so her parents had always said.

That Jack had once been associated—even briefly— with the family from the other side of the tracks had made him completely off-limits.

It felt good to be older now. Mature. Beyond caring about high school cliques and the subtle social structure that existed even within her own family. In twelve more months she could leave and never look back.

A young doctor with curly auburn hair slipped into the room, and Mei shook off her thoughts.

Jasmine immediately sat up straight. "Dr. Kerber—is something wrong? Is Cade all right?"

"First you, young lady." A flicker of a smile softened the woman's stern expression. "Your CT scans, X-rays and labs show no indication of internal bleeding, no fractures. Everything seems to be normal...other than a mild wrist sprain and some minor lacerations, scrapes and bruises."

"I'm free to go?"

"Yes, but I still want someone to be with you for the next forty-eight hours. You experienced quite a fall, and head injuries can still fool us no matter what the tests say."

"She lives with my cousin Arabella Michaels," Mei interjected. "Supervision won't be any problem at all."

"Good, good." Dr. Kerber looked down at the clipboard

she held in the crook of her left arm. "The nurse will be here in a bit to give you a tetanus shot, Jasmine, some going-home instructions regarding your sutures and warning signs of any head injury complications. I'd guess that you are going to be pretty stiff and sore for a few weeks, and you will probably experience headaches. Do you have any questions for me?"

"Just—"

"About Cade. I know." The doctor smiled. "He signed a permission form so I could share his information with you." She shook her head in wonder. "Given the distance of the fall and the massive weight of the boulders that went down with the two of you, it could've been so much worse. All I can say is that God must have been with you both. You not only survived but missed serious head and spinal cord injuries—all too common in this kind of accident."

"God *was* with us." Jasmine closed her eyes briefly. "I've never prayed so hard in my life—especially afterward when Cade was bleeding so much."

Dr. Kerber glanced again at her clipboard. "He wasn't quite as lucky as you, I'm afraid. He has a severely sprained ankle and significant, deep bruising. It took ten sutures to close up that laceration on his head and another eight on his arm. He also has a severe concussion and some mild confusion, so I'm keeping him here for observation for a day or two."

"A concussion?" Jasmine paled and grabbed for Mei's hand. "That sounds bad."

"I think he'll be fine, but I just don't want to take any chances. After he's discharged, I'd strongly recommend that he stay away from contact sports, rodeos or any other activity that might place him at risk for a second head injury."

A tear trickled down Jasmine's cheek. "We were supposed to get married next month on Christmas Eve."

The doctor smiled gently. "Don't worry. Give him a few weeks to heal and you'll never guess that he'd had such a close call."

Mei freshened up in the ladies' room at the hospital, then drove to her mother's home on Bluebird Lane, at the northwest edge of town, and parked out in front. Lisette Clayton stepped onto the wide porch of the two-story brick house before Mei could reach the front door.

"Hi, Mom."

Widowed for years now, she still wore her silver hair in a short, perfectly coiffed style, and always dressed elegantly. Today, her gold necklace and hoop earrings picked up the subtle tones of her champagne cashmere sweater set and matching slacks. As usual, her French manicure was flawless.

She hugged Mei briefly, then scooped up Albert, the fluffy white Maltese dog at her feet. "I was surprised to hear you'd decided to come now instead of waiting until Christmas."

"Change of plans," Mei said, choosing her words carefully.

"Well, do come on in. I can't believe it's this cold already, and it's only the first of November." A wry smile briefly touched Lisette's mouth. "I thought you'd arrive much earlier, so I had your cousin cater our lunch today. She dropped it off before she left for Denver."

"Arabella?" Mei felt her stomach rumble in anticipation. "The pies she brought to Grandpa's funeral luncheon were incredible."

"I'm glad she opened a business that matches her talents. I had her bring pastries for our breakfast, too. I'm not much of a cook anymore."

"It's a lot of bother when you're on your own." Mei shouldered out of her crimson down jacket as she stepped into the marble-floored entryway and tossed it onto the fanciful Victorian settee she'd loved as a child. She took off her shoes, and followed her mother down the central hall leading past the formal living room, parlor and dining room to the spacious kitchen. "I—oh, *wow.*"

Nothing seemed familiar as she stepped into the room and surveyed the rich, dark cherry cabinets and granite countertops. French doors now opened up to a snow-covered patio and, beyond, a charming, snowy view of Silver Creek.

"When did you do all of this?"

"After your grandfather's funeral in July." Lisette shrugged. "Some of my investments have been doing quite well, so I thought I'd do a few upgrades."

"It's beautiful."

"Do you mind what I've done?" Lisette's expression turned pensive. "I've kept the rest of the house the same since your father died."

Remembering how distant and sad Lisette had been since Dad's car accident, Mei smiled. "You deserve a home that makes you happy, Mom."

"I don't suppose Lucas will care either way." Lisette's voice still held a hint of bitterness at the mention of her son's name, even after all this time.

Mei was already a college sophomore when Lucas hit his high school senior year, so she hadn't been around for the rebellious phase that had put him and their parents at constant odds. As far as she knew, he hadn't been home since their father's funeral.

Lisette started a pot of hot water and set a basket of assorted teas on the counter. "Did you have car trouble?"

"No. I stopped to walk on one of the trails and came upon an accident. I lent a helping hand and it took longer than expected. So...what did Arabella make us?" Mei added with a bright smile, hoping to shift the topic away from a side of the family her mother had detested for years.

Lisette studied her closely. "What happened? Anyone we know?"

Mei held back a sigh. "Jasmine Turner. And...um, her fiancé, Cade."

"Cade. Cade *Clayton?*" Lisette's nostrils flared. "I heard about their so-called engagement over the summer and couldn't believe such foolishness."

Mei just shook her head slightly, knowing it would do no good to argue.

"Couldn't Arabella go to the hospital and deal with them?"

"She left for Denver, remember?"

Lisette snorted. "If you ask me, your cousin needs a tighter rein on that girl."

Mei closed her eyes briefly, wishing she hadn't mentioned the accident up on the trail. When would she ever learn? She should've known it would set her mother off. "Jasmine is of legal age and Arabella has no say, really. It's not like she's her mom."

"Well, Jasmine ought to respect the woman who took her in and kept a roof over her head these past few years. And of all people—letting her marry a son of Charley Clayton is just unbelievable."

"I—" Mei faltered to a stop, unable to find any words to defend her infamous uncle Charley. He was widely known as a lazy, disagreeable man who had claimed to have "back injuries" for years to collect disability. If he'd ever had a long-term job, no one in town could remember it.

"Your great-uncle Samuel spawned a family of trouble-makers, and his son Charley is one of the worst."

Apparently the animosity between the two sides of the family hadn't changed in all the years Mei had been away. "Cade and his half brother Jack aren't anything like the others. Jack isn't even a blood relation to the Claytons."

"Blood relation or not, those boys are associated with Samuel's side of the family." Lisette's voice turned to ice. "Jack was one of the boys who tried to ruin your brother's reputation in high school, remember? Imagine, him daring to say Lucas got some lowlife girl pregnant."

"I always figured Vincent was behind the rumors."

"You can be very sure it wasn't just him who spread those lies." Lisette's mouth twisted with distaste. "I shudder when I remember that you had a crush on Jack in high school. Of course, you were young and *very* foolish back then."

Mei flinched. "You need to let go of the past, Mom. Whatever anyone did or didn't do, it was a long time ago. High school–aged kids sometimes do stupid and thoughtless things."

"Young or old, that family is wicked, from Samuel on down." Lisette gave an unladylike snort. "Cade's ridiculous wedding to that girl is just another case in point. Poor judgment, impetuous behavior. It just doesn't end."

"Jasmine says Arabella, Brooke and Vivienne were against it at first, but now they've come around and plan to help out with the wedding."

"So none of your cousins are thinking straight, either." Lisette offered a thin smile. "That's one wedding I'll be sure to miss."

Probably a good thing, for all concerned.

His coat clipped in his usual fluffy puppy cut, Albert looked harmless, but he automatically bared his teeth when Mei inadvertently got a little too close. She darted back a step.

"Silly puppy," Lisette crooned, giving the grumpy little furball an affectionate hug. "Albert doesn't like company."

"Or family members." After attacking Grandpa George's ankle during an Easter dinner, Albert had been dubbed "The Grandpa Bitin' Dog." With good reason. "Has he bitten anyone lately?"

"Only my last cleaning woman," Lisette said with a dismissive wave of her hand. "And Albert was right about her because she certainly wasn't very dedicated. She quit that *very day*."

Mei smothered a laugh at her umbrage. "You're just lucky the woman didn't sue."

"*She's* lucky that I gave her a good reference." Lisette ruffled her companion's soft ears. "You're welcome to your old room upstairs, or you could use one of the cottages. Aspen has already been winterized for the season, but Silver Bells has a better furnace."

Mei's heart lifted at the offer. "A cottage would be wonderful, Mom."

The pretty little rental cottages were set in a stand of pines at the far end of the property along Silver Creek, barely visible from the main house. They'd been part of the quaint resort run by the previous owners, though the other cottages had been torn down long ago.

"You can have it for the year you'll be here, if you like."

Mei's reason for coming early was to be supportive during her brother's troubles, and being close by without sharing the same roof would be perfect. "I'll be happy to pay the full lease."

"I can't take your money, dear," Lisette protested. "You're my daughter."

"But you'll be losing income from tourist rentals."

Lisette fluttered her fingertips. "I hardly depend on that, as you must know. It's mostly just a bit of a hobby for me."

"At least let me pay half then."

"Even that's too much." She frowned. "Do you even have a job? There aren't many opportunities around here."

"I called the principal here before I left San Francisco. I'll be substitute teaching at the high school."

"Really." Lisette gave her a long, assessing look. "I can't imagine that pays well."

Mei sighed. Both of her parents had pushed so hard, wanting her to try for medical or dental school or even law school. That she'd followed her heart into teaching had been just one more disappointment for them…one more failed expectation. "I'll be fine, really."

"Okay, if you must—a hundred dollars a month. I'll start a little savings account with it, and you can have it all back later."

From the glint in her eye Mei knew it would do no good to argue, even though the cottages rented for more than that for a single night. "Deal. That's awesome, Mom."

"Stay here tonight, and tomorrow you can move into the cottage. One of your cousins called this morning and said she'd stop by to help you settle in."

Surprised and touched, Mei cocked her head. "Vivienne?"

"I think so." Lisette put Albert on a chair and withdrew containers marked Fresh Fruit Salad and Chicken Salad with Grapes and Pecans from the refrigerator, put them on the counter and opened a bakery box of fragrant croissants.

In a few minutes they were seated at opposite ends of the long oak table in the dining room, with the aroma of peach tea wafting in the air.

Mei glanced around at the ornate oak buffet, the lighted glass china hutch filled with fine crystal, the sparkling chandelier. Soft classical music provided a quiet backdrop, just as it had a lifetime ago, when she and Lucas had sat across from each other and their parents had taken the opposite ends of the table.

It had been a time to discuss the day's activities. Report cards. Test grades. Lucas had excelled at everything. He was their parents' biological child, born two years after Mei's adoption as an infant, and he'd been the golden child, the unexpected gift from above. The perfect one.

Intelligent and charming, he'd always been able to talk himself out of trouble. Even during his wild and rebellious phase, he'd been the one who fit in this world.

She might have been far more jealous, as a child longing for acceptance, had he not been so kind to her.

And now, after delaying the moment as long as she could, she had to deliver bad news about Lucas to her already fragile mother. Mei's stomach wrenched, her first bite of Arabella's wonderful chicken salad turning to sawdust in her mouth.

Lisette's fork clattered against her plate, her eyes fixed on Mei's face. "I have the most dreadful feeling that you're going to tell me something I don't want to hear."

Mei had practiced this conversation a dozen times on her way to Colorado. But now the words flew from her thoughts and left her fumbling for a gentle way to deliver the message. "It's about Lucas," she began, moving to the chair next to her mother's.

All color drained from Lisette's face. "Is he…"

"He's missing." Mei took her mother's shaking hands in her own. "But knowing Lucas, he's probably just fine."

"Missing?" Lisette echoed faintly, her eyes locked on Mei's. "That can't be. He called and said he was on some sort of mission in Florida so he wouldn't be able to keep in touch. That's probably it. He's involved with some kind of church and…he's just away."

Mei took a long, steadying breath. "Not a church mission, Mom. Apparently a friend betrayed some drug dealers, so they kidnapped his little boy…trying to force the man's cooperation. Luke is trying to help."

Her eyes filled with pain, Lisette clenched her hands in her lap. "I don't understand. Lucas can't be involved in some drug crowd."

"He's not, Mom. But apparently he rescued the child and then disappeared into the Everglades. The police have no idea where Lucas is, and even a private investigator hasn't had any luck. Maybe he's afraid the local cops are dirty and doesn't know who to trust."

Lisette's eyes welled with sudden tears. "Why doesn't he just come home?"

"I don't know. I just know that people are looking for him."

Lisette closed her eyes and folded her hands, her lips moving in silent prayer.

An uncomfortable feeling crawled through Mei. Though often cool and distant, Mom was still a believer, whereas a childhood of weekly church attendance hadn't instilled strong faith in Mei's heart.

The pastor had often referred to God as Father and referred to God's followers as His children. But with her demanding earthly father and the brusque, dismissive attitude of her grandfather, those images couldn't have been less comforting.

Fathers were loving and kind and patient? Not in her world.

Chapter Four

Jack winced at the sight of his brother as he walked into Cade's hospital room the next day. "Hey, there, buddy. You look like you were in quite a fight."

"With a mountain," Cade grumbled, shifting his weight. He bit back a moan at the painful effort. "But I should be outta here, not laying around like some pansy."

Against the white sheets and blankets, propped up with a pile of pillows, the bruises and scrapes on Cade's face and arms were vivid reminders of how close he'd come to being more seriously injured.

"How's that hard head of yours?" Jack asked.

Cade rolled his eyes. "This is a waste of time. The nurses say they're watching me for concussion symptoms. I could do that just fine at home. If I could find my clothes and my boots, I'd leave."

"The doc says you have quite a concussion, bro. That's nothing to fool around with. Yesterday you weren't sure what day it was or where you were." Jack pulled up a chair and straddled it. "And you can't walk on that ankle for a few days, so you can hardly be working cattle out at the Circle C."

"Cody needs every ranch hand he's got. And I need the money. The wedding—"

"I'm sure he won't let you back on a horse or a four-wheeler until you're safe. Liability issues." Jack tipped his head toward the doorway. "Though I expect you'll be out of here and back in the saddle before you know it."

Cade mumbled something and pulled the covers up to his chin at the sound of feminine voices coming down the hall.

"See," Jack teased, angling a glance at the cartoons playing on the TV mounted on the wall. "If you checked yourself out, you'd miss out on all this fine educational TV *and* all the pretty nurses."

The voices drifted past.

"Does Dad know I'm in here? Not that it matters."

He'd known Cade would ask, with his usual bravado firmly in place, because the subject was still touchy after all these years. But there was no way Jack could make things right. Even a brother as loyal as Jack couldn't replace a father who might not bother to check in on his son.

"You signed the privacy release forms when you were seen in the E.R. The social worker said she called both him and Mom when you were admitted."

Cade closed his eyes briefly. "Neither one has called. Not that it's a big surprise. Have you heard from Mom much since she got married again?"

"Just a brief email or two. She said she hated this town and wished she'd left it long ago for the brighter lights of Denver. Of course, when marriage number three ends, she probably won't like Denver, either."

"I sent her a message a while back, telling her about my upcoming wedding to Jasmine, and she never even replied." Cade was now mature in many ways, but the hint of hurt in his voice over his thoughtless parents was unmistakable. "I'm not sure what's worse—a mom who's too busy to be bothered or a dad who's angry about who I'm marrying and wants me to call it off. He doesn't care about me being happy."

"Maybe he's worried about you."

"Are you kidding? It's all about that same old stupid feud, and you know it as well as I do." Cade scowled. "If Jasmine wasn't living with one of George Clayton's grand-daughters, I'll bet Dad wouldn't say a word. He just flat doesn't care about either of us."

"I think he does in his own way. But it's his loss if he doesn't make an effort. You're a good kid, and you deserve much better."

Cade rolled his eyes. "At least Jasmine thinks so."

"And you have me—world's best brother, right?" Jack teased.

Cade barked out a laugh, then moaned and folded his arms over his belly. "Don't make me laugh, man. These muscles hurt."

The fact that Charley was such a lackadaisical father to Cade, his own flesh and blood, never failed to set Jack's temper on edge.

He'd only been a temporary stepson from long ago, barely a blip on the man's radar, and Jack had never been close to Charley. As a kid without a father figure in his life, he'd started out hoping Charley would be that man for him, but Charley hadn't treated his mother well and had barely given Jack the time of day.

For Cade's sake, Jack had always tried to keep his low opinion of Charley to himself. Was hunger for family one of the reasons Cade had chosen to get married so young?

Heavy footsteps clomped down the hall and pulled to a stop outside Cade's room. At his brother's startled expression, Jack turned toward the door.

Charley and Uncle Pauley walked into the room. Short and burly, with thick necks, heavy jowls and small, piercing eyes set deep in their florid faces, no one could mistake them for anything but brothers. But while Pauley held the part-time, unpaid position as town mayor, Charley laid no claim to a job of any sort and was entirely too proud of how he managed to remain on disability for no good reason.

"So, I hear you're taking it easy here," Charley boomed, nodding at Cade. He and Pauley settled their bulky frames into the two chairs in the room. "Pauley and me were just over at the Cowboy Café for some pie, and thought we'd check in on you."

"Since everyone's talking about the accident, we thought we'd better get the news firsthand," Pauley added, his chest expanding with pride. "I need to know what's going on in this town."

No surprise, there. Pauley did almost nothing in his role as mayor, but he was definitely one for gossip, and he gladly shared it with his kin. When Samuel's side of the family somehow managed to campaign him into office last year, they'd supplied themselves with a pipeline of information.

"I heard Mei Clayton was there on the trail." Disappointment flickered to life in Charley's beady eyes. "I didn't know she'd come back to town."

Jack reined in a surge of irritation. "She was the first one on the scene. She made a dangerous hundred-foot descent to get to Cade and Jasmine, and she provided initial first aid."

"That's a shame. Oh, not about you gettin' rescued and all, boy." He waved a hand dismissively. "But it's real disappointing that she actually showed her face in town again. We hoped she mighta stayed in China, or wherever it is she moved to."

"With George's other grandchildren showing up right along, we were counting on her to skip out." Pauley frowned, pursing his full lips. "Of course, there's that fool brother of hers. I hear he's got himself lost in some Florida swamp, so maybe he'll be the one to break ole George's will."

"I don't think you two ought to be planning on any windfall just yet." Cade pulled himself up in bed. "George's grandchildren are going to earn that inheritance because Arabella and all of the other cousins are planning to meet every stipulation of that will."

Pauley chortled. "So they say. But things happen."

Jack had heard rumors about a few of those "things" over the past few months—events that might have been designed to drive some of the cousins away from town before they fulfilled their required time here. He suspected *none* of them had been accidental.

"Just so you know, fellas, Mei is here to stay," Jack said. "I'll take great exception to anyone who tries to cause trouble for her. And—" he leveled a look at each of them in turn "—I'll know who to come after."

"I have no idea what you mean, boy." Charley swiveled in his seat to look up at Jack, the veiled mockery in his voice coming across crystal clear. "Cause trouble? We only *hope* those spoiled, self-serving cousins slip up because they don't deserve to have that inheritance given to them on a silver platter. By all rights, at least half of George's wealth should have belonged to Samuel and to us."

"But we surely aren't going to do anything illegal to get it all back," Pauley added with a smirk. "No sirree. That uppity side of the family always blames us for anything that goes wrong…but that just shows what kinda fools they are."

At a soft knock on the door, they all looked toward the door.

Mei, nearly hidden by a giant bouquet of yellow, orange and white flowers of some kind, stepped inside. "Hi, Cade." She shot a surprised look at the other three men. "I…um…see you have company."

She dropped her gaze to the flowers as she settled them on a shelf under the window and adjusted the big yellow bow fastened to the vase.

Pauley elbowed his brother. "Maybe we'd better get on our way. I told Vincent I was gonna meet up with him about now."

Pauley and Charley lumbered to their feet, nodded at Cade and shot a look of pure dislike toward Mei. They left without another word.

"Oh, my," she murmured as their footsteps receded down the hall. "I'm sorry—I didn't mean to interrupt."

"Company's a good thing," Jack said, hoping he could make her smile. "Especially when it's someone who risked her own safety to help my brother."

"Anyone else would have done the same."

"By rappelling down a cliff face? I doubt that."

"I just happened to be at the right place at the right moment, I guess." She darted a quick, uncertain glance at him, then turned her attention to Cade. "This is all they had in the grocery store floral section, so I hope you like Thanksgiving colors." She pulled a green Randolph's Pharmacy bag from her purse. "And here are some magazines."

Her silky black hair swung forward when she leaned over the bed rail to rest a hand on one of Cade's, hiding her expression from Jack's view. "How are you doing, cowboy?"

He blushed. "I surely don't need to be here. But thanks—that was real nice of you, coming by like this. Jasmine will love the flowers when she comes in."

"I saw her after church, actually, with Arabella and the triplets. I told her that I'd stop by now, and she'll be coming after she helps with Sunday dinner."

"You are coming to the wedding, right?" he asked earnestly. "Jasmine said you hadn't heard about it 'til we saw you on the trail yesterday."

"I guess I've been out of the loop. I...don't make it back here much. My grandfather's funeral was the last time."

Digging his elbows into the mattress, Cade hiked himself higher in the bed. "Sorry about your grandpa."

A shadow crossed her delicate features, though as far as Jack had seen of him, George Clayton Sr. hadn't been a kindly man. Difficult, controlling and power hungry were the words most of the townsfolk used to describe him.

Mei nodded. "Thanks, Cade."

"Hi, everyone. Doesn't he look good? I can't believe it!" Jasmine flitted through the doorway and hurried to the bed to drop a kiss on Cade's cheek. "Arabella let me come over right away because I was just too nervous to stay home. Wow—look at those beautiful flowers."

Cade chuckled, and Jack found himself smiling at the joy she emanated. No matter how foolhardy their marriage plans were, no one could deny that Cade and his young fiancée were hopelessly in love.

Jasmine slid her hand into his. "Did you tell them about our Thanksgiving dinner plans?"

"Uh...not yet."

Mei tilted her head. "So you're really going to go through with this?"

"Yep. We started working out the plans last night. Cade and I are putting on a huge Thanksgiving feast this year."

"She still insists that it'll be for both sides of the family," Cade added with a rueful shake of his head. "I'm guessing that it just might be the most memorable holiday ever, if everyone shows up and they all survive."

"What he means is that it's high time everyone got together and got along, after all these years of feuding between the two branches of the Clayton family tree." Jasmine's mouth formed a firm line. "And for all those who think Cade and I are too immature to get married, putting on this dinner is going to prove to everyone that we are mature, capable adults."

Mei's eyes widened. "Oh, dear. Have you discussed this with Arabella?"

"Yes, and last night I called Brooke, Vivienne and Zach, too."

"And they said…"

Jasmine's cheeks flushed. "I admit it took some explaining. But honestly, it's ridiculous to keep up all the hatred—as if the Claytons were the Colorado version of the Hatfields and McCoys, or something." She took a deep breath. "Since I've been living with Arabella, I'm supposedly part of George's 'side,' and Cade is part of Samuel's. Our marriage is…"

"It's going to be a bit like the Clayton version of *Romeo and Juliet,* to add another analogy," Jack said dryly. "With a much better ending."

"Exactly. But after this dinner I expect *everyone* to come to our Christmas wedding and behave."

"Goodness." Mei blinked and fell silent for a moment. "Have you thought about the expense of making such a dinner for so many people?"

"I've figured out the costs to a penny." Jasmine grinned.

"We're using a good share of our wedding money to pull it off, but we figure we're investing in our future."

As happy as she appeared to be, this was only going to lead to trouble, as far as Jack could see. Then again, she hadn't been in the room a few minutes earlier. If she'd overhead Pauley and Charlie, she would be thinking twice about her whole scheme.

"Is this wise?" Jack said tactfully, not wanting to share those unfortunate insights and add fuel to the flames. "There must be a lot of expenses ahead with the wedding."

"Not really. My uncle Jonathan bought my wedding dress, and with all of the poinsettias at the church every year, I won't need to add any flowers there—just my bouquet. Zach's fiancée, Kylie, wants to be a wedding planner, so she's been helping me with a lot of the details for free. And I'm going to ask everyone to bring their digital cameras and take lots and *lots* of pictures. We can crop and edit them on Cade's laptop and I'm sure we'll end up with a wonderful album."

Jack blinked. He'd spent the past few months trying to convince Cade to wait a few more years to get married. When had all of *this* transpired? "You two are more organized than I realized."

"That's what I want to prove. And we also want to be a part of both sides of the family and not ever feel we're caught in the middle."

"Still, everyone ought to contribute something to this dinner. Most families do it that way so one person isn't stuck with all the work." Mei bit her lower lip. "What did my cousins say?"

"Just what you said. Vivienne, Arabella and Brooke have all insisted on bringing food. Not only that, but Kylie's bringing something, too."

"That makes four, and you can count on Lucas and me,

too. I'm not much of a cook, but he and I can buy some of Arabella's wonderful pies."

Concern flashed in Jasmine's eyes. "Have…um, have you heard from him yet?"

"No. But we will. I'm sure of it."

Despite the determination in Mei's voice, Jack could also hear a hint of worry, and from out of nowhere came the sudden impulse to go to her and give her a long, comforting hug.

He forced himself to stay put. "Lucas is one of the most intelligent, resourceful people I've met. He'll probably show up any day now and wonder why on earth anyone worried about him."

"That would be Lucas." Mei gave him a grateful smile that wobbled a bit at the corners. "Though that streak of independence did get him in trouble a time or two when he was younger."

He found himself glancing at her ring finger—no engagement or wedding rings there—and wondering what she'd been doing during the decade since high school. She'd been so beautiful, so shy back then, and though she'd been known as one of the smart kids, she hadn't hung around with any of the cliques as far as he knew.

"I think I'll leave these two kids for a while and have a cup of coffee," he found himself saying. "Would you like to join me?"

Mei's perfect, golden complexion suffused with delicate pink. "N-no…but thanks. I'd really better get going."

She was gone in a flash, leaving a faint scent of lily of the valley in her wake.

Of course she'd say no. What had he been thinking? The past invaded Jack's thoughts, tinged with the painful humiliation that had cut his pride so deeply back then.

The phone call from her hostile mother.

The visit from her father.

Both had been beyond irate after hearing an unfounded rumor about a relationship between Jack and their precious daughter.

No, he'd been put in his place back then, and the princess clearly felt she was out of his league still.

Maybe they'd bump into each other at Thanksgiving and Cade's Christmas wedding, but even then he'd be sure to steer clear of her. Whatever small inkling of attraction he felt toward her was a complete waste of time.

"I'll see you two later," Jack said. A small envelope on the floor caught his eye as he stood. He scooped it up, turned it over. "Mei must've dropped this. It has her name on it."

Cade chuckled. "Your legs are twice as long as hers. I'll bet you can catch up before she even gets to her car."

"That was certainly awkward," Mei muttered to herself as she zipped up her jacket and walked down the sidewalk toward the hospital parking lot.

She'd expected to see only Cade there, not his brother. And seeing the reaction of Jack's stepdad and his uncle Pauley when she stepped into Cade's room had been nothing less than humiliating. They'd both shot a venomous look in her direction and then they'd practically bolted for the door. What was it with these people?

She'd been gone ten years. She'd never been a player in any part of the ridiculous family feud even when she had lived here. And sure—it was obvious that Samuel and his kin would like to see Grandpa George's estate go to them. But shooting evil glances at her was hardly—

"Mei. Wait up."

She shivered and turned toward the all-too-familiar

face. Was he upset by her interruption up in Cade's room and the way his other relatives had taken off?

"You dropped something."

She eyed the envelope in his hand. MEI CLAYTON was written on the outside in block letters. "What is it?"

"It looks like an invitation. Maybe someone is holding a wedding shower for Jasmine or something."

"If it is, I'll be happy to attend." But a crawling sensation moved up her arm as she started to accept it, and she withdrew her hand.

Her thoughts flashed back to high school, when she'd found similar notes with block lettering that had been stuffed through the vent in her hallway locker. The contents of those notes had haunted her for months. But surely history wouldn't repeat itself after all these years. All of those kids back in school were adults now, and they had to be beyond such immature and hurtful behaviors. Weren't they?

"What's the matter?"

She felt a wave of revulsion. "I don't want it. I don't even want to open it."

He cocked his head and searched her face. "You've received something like this before?"

She nodded. "High school. More than once."

"Is it a threat? If it is, we need to address this. Now."

"I'm sure it isn't even signed," she said matter-of-factly.

"Do you know who it's from?"

She shook her head slowly, unable to take her eyes off the envelope in his hand.

"If you won't open it, how about letting me take a look?"

Humiliation swept through her. "I'd rather you didn't."

"Please."

She sighed heavily. "Read it if you want to. But there's

nothing you can do about it. Just rip it up and throw it in the trash."

His gaze fastened on hers, he slid a fingernail under the flap and lifted out the small card inside. He read it. Then slowly looked up at her.

She forced herself to meet his gaze, fearing what she would find. Pity. Disgust. Knowing that he'd just read what she'd been told in similar notes years ago—that she was an outsider here and always would be. A stupid, anonymous note would mean nothing...except it confirmed how she'd always felt around her grandfather, her cousins and the people in this town. Lonely.

Instead, a muscle worked at the side of his jaw and his eyes blazed with anger. "This is trash, Mei. Pure and simple. You need to at least show it to Zach so he knows that someone resents you this much."

"How would that help? It's not signed, right? It therefore isn't worth Zach's time."

"But now it isn't just some vicious, immature person trying to hurt you. Now there's an inheritance at stake," he argued. "Over a million dollars and a lot of prime Colorado real estate, from what I hear. What if this threat escalates?"

She suppressed a shiver. "I'm not the only one they can go after to break the will."

"But Brooke, Vivienne and Zach have been here longer, so they are more established now...and Arabella has been here all her life. That leaves you and Lucas as the most likely targets—except your brother is out of reach for the time being."

She nodded slowly. "Do whatever you want."

"But it's not just the inheritance. Someone is trying to make you feel unwanted, to drive you away from your own family, and that just isn't right. You need to discuss this with your mom and work things out. It would be better than letting some little piece of your heart wonder if these notes are true."

Though she hadn't intended to waste a glance at the typewritten note, her gaze dropped of its own accord. As before, every letter was capitalized—and she didn't even have to read the whole thing to realize she'd been right.

She knew every word by heart, because she'd gotten this message before.

YOU DON'T BELONG HERE. YOU NEVER DID. YOU SHOULD GO BACK WHERE YOU BELONG AND NEVER, EVER COME BACK OR SOMEDAY YOU'LL BE SORRY.

Chapter Five

Mei opened up another cardboard box and sighed as she glanced around the rental cottage. There were at least another five boxes left, and she hadn't even begun to work in the kitchen. "I can't tell you how much I appreciate you helping me move in, Viv. You could've found more enjoyable ways to spend a Sunday afternoon."

"We're all just so glad you came back early," Vivienne Clayton said with a quiet smile that emphasized the deep dimple in her left cheek. "We don't get to see each other very often."

"And not even when we were kids." Mei had few illusions about the depth of the relationships she'd had with her five cousins while growing up. Painfully shy, bookish and awkward, she'd been last chosen no matter what the playground games were in grade school and too reticent to participate in any high school activities and sports later on. She'd always felt like an outsider. The one who didn't fit in.

She knew Vivienne's enthusiasm was based on relief that one more cousin had shown up to meet the terms of their grandfather's will. But that was fine. Mei was a big girl now. She didn't expect close relationships to bloom where none had existed before.

"I really appreciate your call last week about my brother. I came as soon as I could because I didn't want Mom trying to deal with his disappearance alone."

Lifting an emerald green silk blouse from a box, Vivienne put it on a hanger and fastened the top two buttons. "How did she take the news?"

"Despite the friction between her and Lucas, she's certainly worried." Mei managed a faint smile. "My mom is a master at keeping her emotions in check in front of others—even family—until she suddenly has a big meltdown."

"Poor thing. I don't think she has many close friends. Maybe you can encourage her to become more involved. The Church Care Committee is always looking for new members."

Mei folded a sweater and put it into a dresser drawer. "She changed after Dad died. She's so withdrawn."

Vivienne pulled another blouse from the box and hung it in the closet. "I can't imagine my life if Cody and I broke up—not that it will ever happen." The glow in her eyes and the warmth in her soft, lovely voice confirmed how devoted she was to her fiancé.

"You two are very lucky," Mei murmured. "It isn't often that someone finds their perfect match."

Vivienne laughed. "It took me a while to realize it, though."

Mei lifted an eyebrow. "Cody Jameson is one very good-looking cowboy, as I recall."

"And the nicest, most thoughtful man I've ever met." Vivienne removed a silk shawl from the packing box. "Are you sure you don't want to stay in the main house? I mean, this cottage is lovely, but it might be kind of lonely."

"Mom offered, but it's better that she and I have our own space." Mei opened another cardboard box, one of a dozen she'd crammed into her Blazer for the trip to Colorado. "You haven't lived here since high school, either. Was it hard to come back?"

A small, secret smile lit Vivienne's eyes. "I thought leaving ranch country for the bright lights was my ultimate dream. Little did I know."

"It wasn't?"

Laughing, she flapped a hand in casual dismissal. "I loved attending Le Cordon Bleu, and making sous chef at a fancy New York restaurant was cool."

"It must have been."

"But…" Vivienne's big blue eyes took on a dreamy expression. "Believe it or not, falling for a rancher and cooking for cowboys has proved to have a lot more appeal. Who would've thought?"

Storybook happy endings were so far outside Mei's realm of experience that she felt a twinge of longing. An image of Jack slipped into her thoughts, but she quickly shoved it aside. She'd never met anyone else who could give her just an offhand glance and make her shiver clear to her toes. But he'd never shown a glimmer of interest in her and that wouldn't change.

"Daydreaming about finding some handsome cowboy while you're here?" Vivienne teased.

Mei shook her head. "There'd be no point. I'm leaving town in exactly eleven months, twenty-nine days. But I'm really happy for you, Viv."

"That's so sweet of you. I don't think we've actually sat down for a good talk in years."

Not ever, really, and Mei found herself enjoying the opportunity. "Seeing everyone at Grandpa George's funeral last July was surreal, the way we've all changed so much since high school."

"I wish Lucas had come, though." Vivienne reached for Mei's hand and held it tight. "We've all been praying for him. God is with him. I'm sure of it."

Mei nodded, unable to find the right words in response. What would it be like to have the complete faith in God's presence that Vivienne and Mom seemed to share? Mei prayed, but whether God ever chose to listen to her was another matter.

"I'll help you put away your groceries, and then I'd better be off. I have to get back to the ranch." Strolling to the island separating the living room from the little kitchen, Vivienne started shelving canned goods in the pantry cupboard.

Mei wiped out a cupboard and began shelving an array of spices. "At first I thought the stipulations of Grandpa's will were crazy."

"I agree. But," Vivienne added with a twinkle in her eye, "coming back here brought Cody and me together, so I'd be the last person to complain."

"Strange, isn't it? Grandpa George never showered love on anyone while he was alive. And yet, the stipulations of his will have led four of his grandchildren to someone they love very much."

"He'd roll over in his grave if he knew he'd inadvertently played cupid. Maybe you're the next target," Vivienne teased. "One perfect man, coming up!"

Mei rolled her eyes at that. She'd been painfully shy and withdrawn as a child. And romance? She'd never been lucky in that department at all.

Vivienne tipped her head. "Well…?"

"I'm heading back to San Francisco the minute my year is over. The last thing I want are ties to this town."

"We heard you went to China a while back. Did you enjoy it?"

"Loved it. I taught in an American school for a year and traveled the country whenever I could." At the gentle, knowing expression in Vivienne's eyes, Mei sighed. "And yes, I did try to trace my roots, just out of curiosity. No luck."

"It sounds like a great adventure, though."

"The country has a rich history, and the scenery was incomparable. I loved the students—bright, polite and just so eager to learn. But afterward I found a job in San Francisco, and it's the best I've ever had. The principal says she'll welcome me back as soon as I'm finished here."

Vivienne smiled warmly. "Good for you."

"I'm just glad I kept up my Colorado license so I can teach here."

"Wow." Vivienne's voice was filled with awe. "I've heard turnover is rare in the schools around here."

"Mrs. Sanders had twins and is out for the rest of the school year."

Vivienne's eyes twinkled. "You'd think the principal would've planned a little further ahead for a sub."

"They had one, but he fell on ice and broke a hip."

Vivienne gazed at her. "I'll bet your mom is happy to have you back home for a while."

"In her own way, maybe." Mei debated about telling her cousin about the note she'd received. But what would be the purpose? Vivienne couldn't do anything about it. And, she admitted to herself, it would be embarrassing to reveal that someone thought she deserved such a hateful message. "So...any interesting news around here?"

Vivienne shrugged. "Vincent was fired by the local mine last summer. You probably heard that Uncle Pauley is the unpaid part-time mayor now—a fact that gives me chills. I just hope the town treasurer is watching the purse strings. And far as I know, Uncle Charley still hasn't worked a day in *years.* How he still gets away with being on disability and playing golf on the weekends I'll never know."

Mei nodded. "My mother can barely tolerate any of them."

"You do know about the big romance, right? Jasmine and Cade?"

"I saw them on a hiking trail yesterday and went to the hospital with them after they took a bad fall into a ravine."

Vivienne gasped. "Are they all right?"

"Jasmine is back at Arabella's already. Cade had a concussion, and the doctor is keeping him a day or two." Mei closed the canister. "Jasmine told me about their wedding plans."

"Arabella has tried to dissuade them, believe me. To be honest, I have never trusted Pauley, Charley *or* their kids. But Cade has turned out to be a pretty decent guy, and his brother, Jack, has actually tried really hard to talk Cade into waiting, too." Vivienne pursed her lips. "Maybe there's even a glimmer of good in Jack…though I seriously doubt it. He ran with Vincent back in high school, and in that family, anything they do is self-serving. Vincent is *despicable.*"

Jack hadn't seemed that way to her, but Mei bit back a retort. Vivienne's unexpected friendliness was a precious beginning, a step toward the acceptance Mei had craved all her life. The last thing she wanted now was to start a disagreement. "Why don't Cade and Jasmine listen to reason?"

"They're both of legal age and you've never seen a couple more determined to tie the knot. The only thing we can do now is try to be supportive of them and pray that they'll be happy."

"It's too bad that they won't at least wait until after college."

"I know." Vivienne sighed. "But Jasmine does plan on culinary school, and Cade wants to be a physician. I just hope it all happens."

"Can you imagine the debt they'll incur if Cade does go to medical school?"

"Jasmine's uncle—Dr. Turner—plans to help them with tuition and a place to live. And with Cade's low income as a ranch hand, he should qualify for financial aid as an undergrad. They seem motivated to make their dreams happen."

Mei sighed as she poured a five-pound bag of flour into a canister and snapped on the lid. So there would be a family wedding, after all, and everyone would surely attend—especially Cade's brother, Jack.

While driving to Colorado she'd had hours and hours to mull over the past and think of all the reasons why she didn't want to move back.

Somehow she hadn't even considered the fact that Jack McCord might be in town. But as a search-and-rescue worker, he probably spent his time in the mountains, and she'd be at the high school every day. Because their paths would rarely cross, she wouldn't have to contend with the stirring of old, foolish feelings.

All would be well. She would teach school. Spend time with her mother. Guard her heart. And then surely, the year ahead would be no trouble at all.

Chapter Six

Mei's first day of school passed in a blur.

Now, as a final group of students streamed through the door for her two o'clock environmental science class, Mei sent up a silent prayer of thanks for the absent Mrs. Sanders, who had written out lesson plans through May.

Preparation for her biology and geology classes had kept Mei busy until eleven last night, but luckily Mrs. Sanders had scheduled a guest speaker in environmental science today. Frederick Miller, a local wildlife biologist, would be visiting for five lectures, a field trip and an evening parent program during November.

A shrill bell sounded out in the hallway. The final stragglers shuffled into the classroom and slumped into the remaining open seats with a thud of backpacks on the polished hardwood floor.

Mei leaned against the front of her desk with a clipboard and attendance roster cradled in the crook of her arm. "I'm Ms. Clayton, and I'll be your substitute teacher until the end of the year."

She took attendance, then made a quick call on the intercom to report two absences.

"I grew up here, but I've been away since high school."

She smiled, knowing it was best to set aside curiosity at the very start. "I don't look *quite* like the rest of the Claytons because I was adopted from China as a baby. Since I was curious about my heritage, I spent a year teaching in China, then I moved to San Francisco and have been teaching there until now."

A girl in the front row—Ashley—looked up from picking at the bright red polish on her nails. "Why would anyone leave California to live *here?*"

The frizzy blonde next to her—Gina Meier—rolled her eyes. "I heard a bunch of you Claytons were *forced* to come back, 'cause nasty ole George Clayton croaked and you all want to get your hands on his stupid inheritance."

Mei felt the blood drain from her face at the girl's snide tone. "Excuse me?"

Gina turned to her classmates with a look of triumph. "My mom is Vincent Clayton's second cousin, and he told her so. He oughta know."

"That's hardly a topic for discussion here," Mei chided.

An ugly crimson flush of anger worked up Gina's neck, but she didn't respond.

A Latino boy raised his hand. "When is our class field trip?"

"Good question, Ricardo. It'll be Friday, November 14. Our speaker should be here any minute, and he'll discuss the details, I believe." She looked down at the notepad in her hand. "All right, then—"

When all of the faces in the room swiveled toward the door, Mei faltered to a halt.

From what the chemistry teacher next door had told her over lunch, Frederick Miller was a kindly old fellow, long past retirement and prone to wandering off topic. She'd been hoping the class wouldn't decimate his good spirits.

But the man in the doorway was definitely no stooped, white-haired gentleman.

Silhouetted by the November sunshine beaming through the row of windows along the opposite side of the corridor, she could see he had to be a good six feet or more, with broad shoulders and an upright, military bearing suggesting that he wouldn't suffer fools or difficult teens gladly.

She sighed with relief…until he strode into the room. And then her wayward heart dropped straight to the floor.

The look of shock on Mei's face had to echo his own.

The incident up on the trail with Jasmine and Cade had been surprising enough. Who would ever guess that he'd encounter the likes of Mei Clayton during a rescue on some mountain trail? And now, what was she doing *here?*

Jack tipped his head to acknowledge the students as he strolled to the front of the class. "Hey there, stranger," he said in a low tone. "I never expected to see you here."

"I-I'm a substitute teacher." Her dubious gaze dropped to the Clayton County Forest Service badge on the pocket of his dark green shirt, then back up to his face. "Wh-where's Fred?"

"He transferred to Denver two weeks ago."

"Y-you're *sure?*"

He nearly chuckled at her flustered response. "My office is a cabin roughly the size of a double garage, so I can safely say that he's not here any longer."

"*You're* here to speak?"

Her obvious doubt about him was clear, calling back once again a time he'd tried to forget. Mom's short-lived marriage to Charley Clayton had been just another one of her desperate, brief bids for marital security, but he and Cade had been branded forever by that association—and not in a good way. Mei's obvious reaction made that plain even now.

He swept the old memories aside. "This is the environmental science class, right?"

"Yes…"

"And Fred was scheduled five times during the next three weeks."

She nodded.

"So I'm taking his place. Is that a problem?"

"I—I thought you did search and rescue." A pretty pink flush tinted her delicate face, just as it had at the hospital. "Or that you were…some sort of high-country guide."

"I do both at times. But this has been my real job for the past six years. I worked out of an office at the other end of the county until a few weeks ago."

From her expression he could see more questions were forming in her mind, but they were still standing in front of a class of curious teenagers and this wasn't the best place to answer them. "Those kids are probably wondering what's going on," he added. "So maybe I should get started."

"But have you ever…" She hesitated, then cleared her throat and turned toward the class. "Our speaker is here, and I think I'd better let him do his own introduction so he gets it exactly right."

Smooth save.

"I'm Jack McCord, Clayton County Wildlife Biologist. Most of you have probably seen the local office on Bluebird Lane. It's a set of two cabins, actually—the second one houses whatever biologist works here."

His peripheral vision caught the look of surprise on Mei's face. Apparently she hadn't paid any attention to the cabins across the creek from her mother's rental cottages, but he'd certainly noticed Mei the day she moved in.

"Some of your faces are familiar," he continued. "Jon and Tom, you did a fine job with your Eagle Scout projects restoring the trail leading to Lily Lake. I've seen others on the trails. I hope that by the end of this unit you'll all want to become even more involved in the preservation of our beautiful Rockies."

"Maybe you could tell them how you became a biologist," Mei whispered.

Jack nodded. "I started out like a lot of you—I loved hiking, fly fishing and mountain biking. Anything that kept me outside. As a high school senior, I worked as a fishing guide and later became a high-country hunting guide. Only I found I was more interested in studying wildlife than shooting at it. Guiding is how I paid for college. Can any of you name some endangered species in Colorado?"

A girl in the front row looked up from the doodles she'd been drawing in her notebook. "Whooping crane."

"Yes."

Jon leaned back in his chair and grinned. "Black-footed ferrets."

"Exactly right. They were the topic of my Master's thesis, as Jon knows, because he spent last summer working with me as an intern. Anyone want to guess how many species in Colorado are endangered?"

Silence.

"The number varies as some species are added and others are taken off." He reached into the leather briefcase he'd laid on the front desk and withdrew a stack of handouts. "That question is number one on the assignment I have for you."

He handed them to Mei, and she distributed them as he continued to talk. "You'll be picking an endangered species and then studying the preservation of its habitat."

A collective round of groans rose from the class.

He grinned. "Hold on, it's going to be cool. We're even going up into the mountains to collect data for your paper. I want this project to inspire *all* of you to want to care more about your environment."

Roughly half the class was paying attention. Others were affecting extreme boredom, and some were doodling on the handout. That was nothing new. He'd been one of those doodlers himself back in high school.

Then Jack reached into his front pocket and gently lifted Maxwell up so the little sugar glider could hook its paws on the upper rim of Jack's pocket and sleepily look out into the classroom.

It took less than five seconds for an electrified response to sweep through the class, and now everyone was at rapt attention, whispering and pointing.

"What is it, Mr. McCord?"

"Does it bite?"

"Is it a hamster?"

"A baby squirrel?"

"No, stupid," someone hissed. "It's a gerbil."

"Look at the black-and-white stripes on its face. It's a baby badger."

He ignored them all and started circulating through the room. "After you finish your projects, you'll set up displays for parent night. You'll get to stand by your display and answer questions as visitors walk around."

As he talked about the projects, Maxwell sleepily slipped down into his pocket, wiggled into a comfy position and went back to dozing. Jack felt Mei's steady gaze, and when he glanced over at her, the tilt of her head and her quizzical expression made him falter. Was she surprised to find that he'd actually finished college and had a career beyond guiding hunters into the high country?

The shrill hallway bell sounded, marking the end of class, but every student stayed seated and at least twelve hands shot up.

He smiled. "I suppose you're wondering about Maxwell."

When a cacophony of questions erupted, Jack held up his hand. "He's a sugar glider. He's nocturnal. Does anyone know what that means?"

Ricardo's hand shot up. "He sleeps during the day."

"Right. I'm babysitting while his owner is out of town. Sugar gliders become very attached to their owners, but the boys are a little better about strangers. I dropped him in my pocket to bring him along so he wouldn't feel lonely while I was gone."

"But what is he?"

"He's a marsupial—so the females carry their young in a pouch, just as kangaroos do. The babies are called joeys, in fact. They live up in the trees and they can glide through the air, from one tree to the next, like flying squirrels."

The class expelled a collective *wow,* clearly enchanted, then the questions came fast and furious. Finally Jack held up both hands, palm out. "I'll see if I can't bring another friend next time. Nature is an amazing thing, guys. I hope you'll appreciate it all the more when this unit is over."

The students left in a scramble of chairs and desks squealing against the wood floors, jostling to get through the doorway with their bulky backpacks, too many bodies at a time.

A few minutes later the room was silent.

Mei leaned against the front edge of her desk, her arms folded in front of her chest and her expression cool. "Seeing you here was…um…quite a surprise. I was expecting someone twice your age."

"I was surprised to see you here, too."

She arched a brow. "Then search and rescue isn't your career."

"Strictly volunteer. But with all of the practice sessions and other meetings, it's practically a half-time job." He handed extra copies of the syllabus to her. "Here you go, in case anyone was absent."

"And you're a wildlife biologist?"

"With a Master's." He sighed. "It's been a long road. I worked my way through school so I could graduate debt-free."

She ducked her head a little to one side, her long black hair shifting like a gleaming waterfall. "That's impressive. Most of the guys in this town just follow in their daddies' footsteps…family businesses and such."

"And do very well. But a lot of them weren't in my shoes. Poverty gives motivation a whole new meaning," he added with a smile. "But I'm sure you wouldn't know about difficult beginnings."

Her jaw dropped. "You think I got whatever I wanted on some silver platter? Or that my life here was *happy?*"

He'd just been making a halfhearted joke about his own background and hadn't meant to insult her, but from the hurt, defensive look in her eyes, apparently he had. "Sorry."

She shifted uncomfortably. "Me, too. Coming back here has made me…oversensitive or something. You did a good job in class today," she added stiffly as she gathered her purse and briefcase. "Be sure to let me know if you need any audiovisual equipment for your next lecture."

She headed out the door, waited for him to leave and then locked the classroom door behind him. Without another word she strode down the hallway with her heels clicking against the floor in a rapid staccato beat.

He watched her go, then turned toward the front entrance, where he'd left his truck out along the curb.

Four more sessions, a field trip and a parent open house meant six more opportunities to see if he could get past Mei Clayton's prickly defenses. Did she have a warm heart hidden behind all of that armor?

With parents like hers, maybe not. But it still might be interesting to try.

Chapter Seven

Lisette poured two cups of hot blackberry tea, rounded the kitchen island and set them on the glass-and-wrought-iron table.

As soon as she sat down, Albert stood on his back legs by her chair and begged to be lifted into her lap. "How was your first day of school?"

"Fine." Mei brought a serving tray of Arabella's raspberry-almond scones, lemon curd and softened butter to the table and settled into a chair facing the double set of French doors.

Lisette moved a scone to her plate, broke off a piece, buttered it and fed it to Albert. "That's not much of an answer, but I can understand that you might well be... disillusioned with your career." Lisette stirred a packet of sweetener into her tea and looked at Mei over the rim as she took a delicate sip. "I've always wondered when you might decide to go back to school and try something... different."

"Like medical school?" Mei asked drily. It was an old, well-worn topic, and one of many that had made living far away from here a pleasant alternative.

Both her parents had wanted her to follow in her dad's

footsteps and become a doctor. They had been all about measuring up and meeting expectations, not simple, unconditional love and acceptance. What would it have been like to be truly loved for exactly who she was? To feel as if she really belonged in this family? She would never know.

The one thing she'd been able to count on was that she always seemed to disappoint her mother in some way, and that had been double for her late father.

Lisette pursed her lips. "I'm sure teaching must be fun, dear. But really, with your intellect there are so many other options out there...and you're still young enough to spread your wings."

Mei felt her blood pressure ratchet up a notch. "Fun isn't exactly the right word. Sometimes it is, but try challenging. Difficult. Rewarding."

"You should add underpaid and underappreciated," Lisette added with a sigh.

"Maybe. But I'm certainly not disillusioned. I think teaching is what I was meant to do." Mei warmed to the subject, willing her mother to understand. "Grady Falls High in San Francisco is amazing. My principal is progressive and supportive, and they have a substantial budget for textbooks and other resources. Every student in the country should be so lucky."

"Lucky?" Lisette sniffed. "To have textbooks? Surely that can't be unusual."

"I've been in many schools where there were only a handful of textbooks in each class, so the students had to share. Grady Falls has been my best teaching experience yet. I can't wait to go back."

Lisette slowly settled her cup onto its saucer. "But you do have a full year here. Maybe you'll find you like being home and want to stay."

Mei's heart twisted with guilt at the veiled hope in

Mom's voice. Sometimes her bitterness and anger were hard to take, but with her husband gone and both children grown and away, she probably was lonely. And Mei hadn't called and written nearly enough.

"I'm glad we'll have this time together, Mom. Do you know what would be fun while I'm here? Finding some way to volunteer in this community. Becoming involved."

Lisette waved a hand dismissively. "Both you and Lucas could've followed in your father's footsteps by taking over your father's medical practice right here in town. You really could've helped the community then, don't you think?"

Mei sighed. Mom really did have a one-track mind. "Lucas loves being a vet. He didn't want to be a doctor."

"No. Being Lucas, he always had to rebel and take the opposite road, no matter what was expected of him. That boy found more ways to be difficult—" Lisette fell abruptly silent, a hand at her mouth and her forehead knit with worry. "I'm still upset with the way he left town and didn't ever bother to come home, but what I wouldn't give to have him back with me right this minute. If it wasn't for that despicable Vincent and those other worthless Claytons, maybe we wouldn't have had that final argument."

Lucas. Where was he now, and why didn't he call? Mei reached across the table and took her mother's hand. "He'll be back soon. I know he will."

Lisette took another sip of her tea, her expression stark. "I pray that it's true."

Unable to sit still any longer, Mei went to stand at the French doors. To the far left, she could see a corner of her cottage through a stand of pines, though those trees hid the view of the opposite side of the creek. "You can't see them from here, but who owns those cabins across the creek from your cottages?"

"The Clayton County Forest Service. Why?"

"Um…just asking." So it was true. Of all the places that Mom could have had rental property, it was right across the creek from Jack McCord.

"One cabin houses the local office, the other is a residence, I believe."

"Really."

"Believe me, I was totally against the state buying that property a few years ago. This area should be zoned residential." Lisette stroked Albert's fluffy white coat. "But you needn't worry. The wildlife biologist who works out of that office is an older man, and it's very quiet over there most of the time. I imagine he's mostly out in the woods counting bears, or whatever those people do."

So Mom hadn't yet discovered the changing of the guard. But once she realized that Jack was her new neighbor, Mei guessed that she wouldn't be just concerned about potential noise.

The incident back in high school, involving the false rumors about Lucas getting some girl pregnant, had been designed to ruin his reputation. Though teenagers could be cruel at that age and there were untold others who could have a grudge against the lofty Claytons, Mom had always been sure that the trouble was caused by Vincent and others on that distant side of the family tree. Even if Jack hadn't been a part of it, he'd forever be associated with those troublemakers in Mom's mind.

And though it was at complete odds with the tenets of her faith, Lisette never forgave and never forgot when it came to protecting her loved ones. She'd despised Jack McCord ever since.

Once again, an image of Jack's face slipped into Mei's thoughts. Coming into a high school class as a speaker wasn't easy, but with his quiet authority, his obvious passion for his career and the whimsical addition of Maxwell the sugar glider, he'd won over the class in less than an hour…and had reminded her of all the ways he'd fascinated her as a teenager, too.

Not that it mattered.

She remembered her mother's rage over those rumors about Lucas and countless other situations involving Samuel's side of the family tree. The situation had terrified her as a child. And even now, Vivienne had expressed deep doubts about Jack.

In this town you were on one side or the other, and it had always been that way. And—she had to admit—it wasn't all based on pettiness and lies. Samuel's side of the family had nurtured a grudge against George's side for decades, and the conniving and plotting between them all had caused endless trouble that just made things worse. It was only by the grace of God that things hadn't escalated to murder by now.

Maybe Jack had held a small corner of her heart all these years. But if she crossed the line into friendship with him, she knew she'd be giving up any chance of building a relationship with her mom.

However, seeing him over and over again in her class was bound to make things even more difficult.

She sighed heavily. Tomorrow she needed to go see Jack and try for some damage control. And then she could only hope for the best.

Wednesday dawned clear and bright, the early-morning sunshine turning the snow around Jack's office into a field of rosy, glittering diamonds.

He checked the contents of his backpack once again, then put it into his Clayton County Forest Service SUV and started toward his office to grab his sunglasses and parka.

A navy Blazer bounced through the deep ruts on Blue-bird Lane and pulled into the lane behind his SUV just as he stepped outside again. He tossed the parka into his vehicle and strolled to the Blazer when the driver opened the door.

He did a double take, his pulse kicking in a couple of extra beats. "Mei?"

She lifted her sunglasses and propped them on the top of her head. "I'm on my way to school but thought I ought to stop by with a warning." She ducked her head, clearly embarrassed. "Just in case. And believe me, there's not a thing I can do about it."

He had a pretty good idea where this was going, but saying so would only embarrass her further. "A bear sighting."

"No."

"Wolf?"

"Uh...no."

"Coyote, then. They come into town now and then. The bears, too."

"None of those." She shivered and wrapped her arms around her middle.

"Do you want to step into my office for a minute and talk about it?"

She hesitated, then glanced over her shoulder toward Silver Creek and nodded slowly. "That might be best. But just for a few minutes."

He ushered her into the cabin housing the Forest Service offices.

Warm and cozy, with a big stone fireplace at one end, its pine-paneled interior walls were covered with maps of the area, posters and charts. The front reception area, with a large desk and several overstuffed chairs, could be rearranged to seat forty for educational seminars, while the rest of the building was divided into two offices and a storage room.

She glanced around. "Very nice," she murmured. "Wasn't this a log home at one time?"

"It was until a few years ago." He waved her toward one of the upholstered chairs, then leaned against the desk. "What's up?"

She shifted uneasily in her chair. "I live on the opposite side of the creek from here."

"I know."

"At the end of my mother's property."

He nodded.

"She thinks Fred Miller still operates this place, and she…hasn't seen you here yet."

"Maybe not. These buildings face Bluebird Lane, not the creek."

She nervously fiddled with her hair. "My mother has isolated herself a great deal since my father's death. She… tends to dwell on the past and sometimes builds things up in her mind. I'm afraid she's not a very forgiving woman."

Tell me about it, Jack thought wryly.

Mei averted her eyes. "I've tried to talk to her, but I'm sure it didn't do a lick of good. So I just wanted to warn you and apologize in advance if she happens to cross your path and says something rude. Truth is, she still associates you and Cade with Vincent and his dad, Charley. They've done some pretty underhanded, awful things to our side of the family over the years. Get her started on *that* topic and you've got a tirade on your hands."

"I think I can handle a few angry words."

"It's not just that. I know you aren't going to believe this, but…" She closed her eyes. "This is so embarrassing."

Deep color suffused her cheeks, and once again he thought about how cute she was when she blushed.

"She…um…thinks I had some sort of schoolgirl crush on you when we were in high school. She still brings it up, apparently under the misapprehension that I'm going to throw myself at your feet or something. I know it sounds crazy—but I'm twenty-eight and she's *still* the most protective parent on the planet. And…" Mei took a deep breath. "She doesn't yet know that you'll be an ongoing speaker in my class. I'll explain it to her, but being Mom, she's probably going to fabricate some sort of romance in her mind. If she ever confronts you and…uh…warns you away from me, I just want to apologize from the bottom of my heart."

Too late.

Apparently Mei didn't know about the incidents in high school when each of her parents had done exactly that. "I understand. Don't worry about it."

Mei gave him a faint, wobbly smile. "Unbelievable, isn't it? Having to worry about my *mother's* behavior? I'm just hoping I can get her out and about more while I'm here. If she'll only start volunteering and socializing more, I think she'll be a lot happier and dwell on the past a lot less."

"I'm sure she will."

Jack gave in to an impulse and reached out to take Mei's hand. It felt so small and delicate in his own that he consciously gentled his touch, then released his grip. "I just hope she realizes how fortunate she is. And you, too."

"Right," Mei scoffed.

"She's blessed to have a daughter who cares about her. And you are fortunate to have a mom who is still so concerned and caring about you. Believe me, not all parents are like that. Personally, I can't even imagine it."

"I…I'm sorry."

"Don't be. Even the worst situations have silver linings, don't you agree?"

"I guess."

"Take Charley, for instance. My mother has married three times, and he was her biggest mistake of all."

Her mouth twitched. "*My* mother would agree with that. Charley isn't exactly her favorite person."

"Wise woman. We all live in the same town, yet as soon as the divorce was final he became the worst kind of absentee father. He rarely followed through on his shared custody times, so Cade would get his hopes up and be disappointed, over and over again. Now, he's irritated about Cade's wedding plans and is sure sharing his opinions… but otherwise, he doesn't much care."

"And you?" Mei murmured.

"He mostly pretended I didn't exist, though that was just as well."

Her eyes filled with compassion. "That's so unfair."

"Still, if Mom hadn't married Charley, she wouldn't have had Cade. And he's one of the brightest spots in my life."

"Is he out of the hospital yet?" she asked.

"Either this evening or tomorrow. The doctors were concerned about brain swelling, which can worsen days after a concussion." He sighed with relief. "But that hasn't happened, and he seems to be back to normal. Seeing him dazed and confused right after the accident had us all worried."

"I'm so glad he's doing well. He's lucky to have you as his brother, Jack."

Her expression grew pensive, and he wondered if she

was thinking about her missing brother. "Have you heard anything from Lucas yet?"

"Not a word. Zach tried working with the police down there, then he hired a private investigator a few months ago. We still don't have any answers. If we don't hear anything soon, I'm going to contact the police department in Florida myself. How could Lucas disappear with that little boy and not leave a trail?"

"I've heard that a person could hide forever in the Everglades and never be found."

"But why? Why wouldn't he go to the police?" Mei's lower lip trembled. "Or why wouldn't he find a way to come home? He'd be safe here."

"I can't say. But I'm sure that P.I. and the detectives down there must be doing everything they can."

She met his eyes. "My mom is a bundle of nerves over Lucas and just won't admit it—which is another reason I thought I'd better stop by. Since Dad died she hasn't handled stress very well. I just wouldn't want her taking it out on you."

"No worries."

Mei wearily looked up at the clock on the wall. "I guess I'd better get to school. I suppose you need to get to work, too…at whatever it is you do. My mom thinks Fred just went off into the woods to count bears."

"Actually, that's exactly what I'm doing today."

She looked startled, then laughed. "Really? Isn't that sort of dangerous?"

"We contract with a local helicopter owner and do aerial surveys for overall population estimates." He smiled. "My biggest danger is getting airsick if we do a lot of circling."

"Sounds like fun—except for the airsick part."

"We also track migration patterns of large game via

radio telemetry, and I've picked up a mortality signal from one of our collars. I need to see where that carcass is so I can go after it."

"You mean you get *out* of that nice, safe helicopter so one of those bears can have you for lunch?"

He grinned. "I hope not."

She gave him a tentative smile. "Be careful, Jack."

He followed her outside, then paused at the door of his SUV and waved as she drove away.

After their last awkward conversation, he never would've guessed that Mei would stop by today…or that her icy shell would melt enough for her to reveal more about herself than he'd known before.

He'd always thought her snooty and privileged, because she'd held herself aloof. But now he knew the truth. She was shy. And with a family like hers, her upbringing had been as difficult as his own, only in different ways.

He smiled to himself as he drove to meet his helicopter pilot at the private airstrip outside of town.

He hadn't been looking forward to fulfilling Fred's commitment to the high school environmental science class, but he definitely would anticipate those classes now.

Chapter Eight

Mei sat at the little pine kitchen table in her cottage with a towering stack of quizzes to grade, ruing her impulse to schedule a quiz in every one of her classes on her second day at Clayton High.

They were all easy, short-answer quizzes, but she'd been eager to find out just where her students all stood so she could get off to the right start. But now, with the output of five classes at twenty to thirty students each staring back at her, she realized it was an impulse she should've ignored.

With a sigh, she forced her gaze back to Gina Meier's environmental science quiz and marked yet another answer wrong.

But once again her gaze bounced right back to the windows facing the creek. She could still make out the outlines of the two cabins across the creek, though dusk had deepened to near darkness.

The lights were still off over there. Where in the world was Jack?

She shivered, remembering his offhand words about counting bears, and mortality signals on collars, and needing to trek into some primitive mountain area to collect a dead animal.

How on earth could someone drag a whole bear back to civilization—and what would happen if its buddies didn't approve? What if he was hurt and unable to make it home?

She corrected the rest of Gina's paper and reached for the next one. Looked outside again. The windows were still dark over there.

Maybe she should call the sheriff's office.

Or maybe she should just get in her car, drive over and see if he was all right. He might have been home all this time—but in a front room of his cabin—or he could be in town, having a leisurely supper at the Cowboy Café, oblivious to her concern.

But if she didn't look in on him, correcting the quizzes was going to take until next Sunday. With a sigh, she tossed her red pen aside, shouldered on her cranberry winter jacket and went outside to start her car.

Lisette materialized out of the darkness, with Albert trotting at her side. "Hello, dear!"

Mei blinked, her heart sinking. "Hi, Mom."

"Where are you heading? It's supposed to start sleeting pretty soon according to the news."

"Um…" She swallowed. "Isn't it too cold out here for Albert?"

"He does fine with his insulated coat. We always go out about this time in the evening." She leaned down to give him an affectionate pat on the head. "If you need groceries, you're welcome to anything in my pantry."

"I just had an errand to run."

"You're still thinking you're in San Francisco, not Clayton. Only the café and the grocery store are open after six, and…" She lifted her wrist, pushed back the sleeve of her heavy jacket and peered at her watch. "The grocery store will be closing in less than fifteen minutes."

"I actually needed to see someone."

"One of your cousins?"

Mei had forgotten just how persistent Mom could be. "No. I'm running over to see the wildlife biologist across the creek. He's…um…speaking in my environmental science class. I'll be back in just a few minutes."

"Oh. Well, then…be careful. The roads could turn to ice anytime now."

Mei sighed, watched her mother disappear into the darkness, then drove slowly down the narrow lane leading past her mother's house. She'd hesitated to say exactly who that biologist was, but perhaps she just should have gotten it over with. Maybe Mom would even surprise her and be nonchalant about the whole thing.

And maybe prairie dogs could fly.

She turned up Bluebird Lane and pulled into the drive that led from the lane to the two cabins. Dark, both of them.

She shivered as she drove to the Cowboy Café, imagining Jack McCord torn to pieces on some mountain trail… or injured, hiding in a cave and praying for help to arrive. He'd certainly seemed capable enough, but bears could be aggressive and there were moose and coyotes and mountain lions out there, too. *Big* things. With sharp teeth. Huge claws. Fearsome antlers.

Turning south on Hawk, she slowed when she crossed Railroad Street and reached the café, peering at the vehicles parked along the street. Pickups, SUVs, cars…it was too dark to discern the colors or read all of the license plates clearly.

A patrol car caught her eye and she pulled in next to it.

"I hope it belongs to you, Zach," she muttered to herself as she walked into the café.

The place hadn't changed much since she'd regularly stopped in after school for a soda or ice cream on her way home from school all those years ago.

The café was deep and narrow, with a long soda fountain and red vinyl swivel stools that stretched along one side, with glass pastry cases positioned every six stools. Usually there were wonderful pies and pastries and incredibly tempting slices of triple-layer cakes in the glass cases on the counter. Heavy square oak tables and sturdy wooden chairs still filled every available space, and the old-fashioned, ornately engraved cash register still sat on the counter near the front door. But the Wurlitzer bubbler jukebox was gone, replaced with a newer model.

This late in the day only a few slices of pie were left and just a handful of people were still here. But unlike the old days, the only person she recognized in the entire place was her cousin Zach—until he shifted his weight on one of the stools at the counter and she glimpsed Jack sitting next to him.

Feeling a little foolish over her earlier worries, she nodded to them both and slipped onto the stool next to Zach. She inhaled the wonderful aromas rising from his hot beef sandwich. "Let me guess. The beef is fork tender, that wonderful, rich brown gravy was homemade and those mashed potatoes never saw the inside of a box."

"And underneath is a slab of homemade bread. It's a wonder I can still fit in my uniform I come here so often."

"It's a nice one," she murmured, tipping her head slightly to read the words on his badge. "How do you like being the deputy sheriff?"

"I like it just fine." He reached around her shoulders

and gave her a quick one-armed hug. "Good to see you, Mei. I heard you were back in town."

"Just since Sunday."

"Jack was just telling me that he's already been a guest speaker in one of your classes at the high school. Small world, eh?"

"It's certainly a small town," she said drily. She leaned forward to see around Zach and saw Jack in the midst of polishing off an order of fish and chips. "I've been worried about you. So apparently the bears didn't have you for lunch?"

"I ended up just doing the aerial counts today. It's going to take a couple men on ATVs to bring in that carcass tomorrow."

She shuddered. "Why do you need it?"

"The state veterinarians will post it—an autopsy, in vet lingo—to determine cause of death, what it last ate, how well it's been nourished and so on."

"Thanks, guys. Great topic while I finish my supper," Zach drawled as he scooped up a fork of mashed potatoes.

A pretty young waitress with a long, curly, golden-brown ponytail came down the back of the counter, a coffeepot in hand, filling coffee mugs and chatting with the rancher types along the way.

She fixed a dazzling smile on Mei. "You must be new in town, ma'am. Would you like a menu?"

"No…I just needed to talk to Zach for a moment."

"Just coffee, then? We still do have a few slices of Arabella's fabulous blueberry pie. How they lasted this late in the day, I have no idea. Flakiest crust you'll ever savor, believe me."

"*Arabella's* pie?" Mei's stomach growled, and she belatedly remembered that she'd forgotten to make something for supper.

The waitress winked. "One slice, coming right up. À la mode?"

The combination sent her stomach into an impatient tap dance. "Sounds perfect. With a coffee, please."

Zach shoved aside his empty dinner plate. "Me, too. I'd hate to see that last piece disappear."

The waitress returned in a flash with the order.

Zach took a bite of pie and closed his eyes in sheer bliss. "Have you two ladies met?"

The waitress looked uncertainly between Mei and Zach, then her eyes widened. "You must be Zach's cousin. From California, right? I'm just so glad to meet you!"

Zach looked at her with such love in his eyes that Mei didn't even have to ask. "And you must be Kylie. Vivienne mentioned that you two were dating."

"Engaged, but we're still working on a date." He reached over the counter and gave Kylie's hand an affectionate squeeze. "I'd opt for next week, but Kylie here is starting up a wedding consultant business, and she's having way too much fun deciding all of the details."

Kylie winked at him. "It's *research,* honey. Remember?"

She topped off Mei's mug of coffee. "This is a small town, but Zach suggested that I could have a local bridal shop and office and also build my business online. You know, to offer accessories, bridal gowns, special orders for bridesmaid dresses and so on. Eventually, I'll be able to do it full-time."

"Sounds like a wonderful idea." Mei smiled at her bubbly enthusiasm as the perky waitress floated away. "You found a wonderful gal, Zach. You're a lucky man."

"I am. Believe me, I know."

Somehow all of his pie had vanished while Mei was

still toying with a second bite of her own. "I did want to ask you some questions, if you have time."

He took a long swallow of coffee, then set aside his mug and swiveled to face her. "What's up?"

"It's Lucas. Mom and I are worried about him because we still haven't heard a word."

"Vivienne told you about the contacts I made with the police department down there, right?"

"And about the private investigator you hired."

He nodded. "The police have hit a brick wall. They say Lucas disappeared without a trace, and they've exhausted every avenue of investigation."

"What have they done, though? Is it enough?" Mei bit her lower lip. "Do they even *care?*"

"They've conducted multiple searches in the Everglades, and they've staked out the area. They also arrested one of the members of the drug gang and interrogated him extensively. Apparently," Zach added with a shake of his head, "that gang wants to find Lucas, too. I just hope the good guys find him first."

Mei drew in a sharp breath.

"I'm sorry, Mei."

"What about the private investigator?" she asked.

"There have been two. One was on the case for more than a month, and then he dropped out of sight. The second one says he's been following some leads but so far, every one of them has come up dry."

"Do…you think—" The rest of the words caught in her throat.

"Do I think something has happened to Lucas?" Zach sighed heavily. "I hope not. The Everglades are beautiful to tourists, but they can be a dangerous place. If he's hiding out there, he's facing danger every day, and he likely still has that little boy with him. Food, safe water, shelter—he has a lot of things to worry about."

But she knew there were other, far more threatening things out there that he was tactfully omitting. "Alligators and snakes."

"I'm afraid so."

"And lowlifes who lose themselves out there to stay outside of the law. I read the news, Zach."

Jack set aside his plate. "I don't mean to intrude, but I couldn't help but overhear. What other agencies are involved in trying to find him?"

"Just the local police."

Jack frowned. "What about the DEA? They sure ought to have an interest in drugs moving through the area."

"I have a feeling they already do, though no one at the police department is willing to come right out and say anything." Zach glanced over his shoulder and lowered his voice. "I think there might be a big investigation going on down there now, and they are trying to spread a very wide net. From the vague hints I received, I'd guess they have undercover guys who have been working this operation for months or even longer, and no one wants to throw it all away."

"But my brother—doesn't he matter?"

"Of course he does. I imagine there are a lot of agents down there who have been alerted to keep an eye out for him. No news is good news, probably."

"Unless he's already dead." Mei shuddered. "Just the thought of those Florida alligators scares me."

Jack flicked an unreadable look at Zach, then met Mei's eyes. "I think you need to stay positive. If no one has seen any sign of him, he's either still well hidden in that area, or he has slipped away unseen. For all we know, he might be a hundred miles away from there by now. Maybe he's even on his way home."

Zach cleared his throat. "That's right."

They were both just trying to comfort her, she could feel it in her bones. But after all the time Lucas had been gone, the chances of ever seeing him again alive were decreasing every day. "You'll call me if you hear anything at all?"

Zach nodded. "Absolutely."

She put a five-dollar bill on the counter and got up to leave, feeling a little ill. Zach gently grabbed her hand.

"I want you to know that everyone at church is praying for him, Mei. We're praying for his safety and his safe deliverance back to this town. God is with him. I'm sure of it."

Chapter Nine

Jack caught up with Mei outside the café. "I'm sorry about your brother. It's got to be awfully hard on you and your mom, wondering if he's all right."

She didn't turn around, but bowed her head, her long, beautiful hair cascading down her back.

"Is there anything I can do?"

She shook her head.

He'd wanted to offer her comfort before. Now he wanted more—to pull her into his arms for a long, sweet kiss. She'd touched his heart clear back in high school, though there had always been barriers between them that he couldn't cross. Yet standing by and watching her suffer, knowing that she probably had no one else to turn to, made his insides clench.

"Mei?" he said softly. She turned toward him as he moved forward and pulled her gently into his arms, tucking her head beneath his chin. "I am so, so sorry."

When she wrapped her arms around him and sank against his chest in response, he closed his eyes briefly at the wonder of holding her close. He felt a shudder course through her and wished he wouldn't ever have to let her go.

If only things were different.

"I do believe what Zach said, with all my heart," he murmured. "A lot of people in this town are praying for your brother, and God is with him every moment. Whatever happens, you can all be so proud of him. He's a courageous, honorable man. Not many people would risk their lives to save that child like he has."

She nodded against his chest. "I—I know."

"And a lot of people are searching for him." Jack took a half step back and lifted her chin with a forefinger to look down into Mei's eyes. "I think he'll be here sooner than you think."

"I hope so. I can't tell you how much. Maybe our parents weren't exactly like those on the old family sitcom reruns I watched as a kid, but Lucas and I were pretty close. At least when we were young. Now I wish we'd kept in touch better as adults."

A sedan drove past and a couple of cowboys came out of the café, joking about some problems out at a ranch. Their voices soon faded away, but Mei had already stepped out of Jack's embrace.

She started walking away from the brightly lit front of the café. "The situation with Lucas has made me think about a lot of things. So much guilt, so much regret."

"You? I can't imagine that."

"It's true. Do you ever feel terrible guilt about something you said or did but there's no way to undo that harm?"

He fell in step with her. "I think everyone does at times."

"There are so many things I wish I could change."

Surprised, he caught her hand and held on. "I cannot picture you doing anything hurtful. To anyone."

She laughed bitterly. "Then looks are deceiving. My

grandpa George was a cold, hard man. I was legally adopted as a baby, but I heard him say more than once that I didn't fit in the family—I'd always just be some foreigner."

Jack drew in a slow breath. "What a terrible thing to say to a granddaughter."

"My dad stood up to him, but the words hurt all the same. I did my best to avoid Grandpa at all costs after that—I barely spoke to him again. Yet—" Her voice wobbled. "And yet, he included me in his will, just like all of the other cousins. I was stunned. It isn't about the land or money—if only a single dollar was involved, it would still mean the same. It's the fact that despite his harsh and hurtful words, I wasn't ignored."

"So he did love you."

"I doubt it. The will was probably set up on the advice of his lawyer for simple equality between each of his children's families. But it still gave me a wonderful gift— the feeling that he didn't totally reject me, after all." She sighed with regret. "Death is a terrible thing, isn't it? I wish I'd been more thoughtful and loving toward him, but now there's no way to go back and say or do the things I should have. All I'm left with is guilt."

"From what I saw of him, George Clayton never made it easy for anyone. Any child would try to avoid someone who was cruel and thoughtless. It must have been scary to hear him say you didn't belong—as if the security of your family could be snatched away. That's heavy stuff for a kid to deal with."

She angled a look up at him. "I'm not even sure why I'm telling you all of this. I've never told another soul," she said quietly. "Thank you for understanding."

He understood, all right.

She had no idea just how hard won his empathy was,

but he'd walked in her shoes. The emotional turmoil he'd dealt with as a child, throughout his mother's brief and sometimes explosive marriages and extramarital relationships, had made his young life a battlefield.

He smiled gently. "You're wrong, though, about never having a chance for amends. Longing for that can be a terrible burden, but prayer has helped me work through a lot of guilt and regrets. And one day, if your grandfather was a believer, you'll see him in heaven and he'll welcome you with open arms." His voice filled with conviction. "And every one of your mistakes and hurts and sorrows will be washed away. For both of you."

She pulled her car keys from her pocket and stopped in front of her Blazer. "I hope so. There are so many things I wish I could say to my brother, too. I want so badly to see him again and set those things straight."

Jack's heart wrenched at the sad and lonely expression in her eyes. He rested his hands on her shoulders, then brushed a swift kiss on her forehead. "You'll have that chance, Mei. I'm sure of it."

The first sound came after midnight, like the softest brush against Mei's front door. Then a whisper of something pawing against the wood.

There was a pause.

Then it came again, a little louder.

Mei sat bolt upright in bed, grabbed her cell phone from the bedside table and listened.

A bear would be loud, purposeful, without regard for subterfuge. If it were this close to the cottage, it would be trying to tear apart the bear-safe trash cans not far from the cabin entrance.

A coyote? Maybe. Coyotes were no longer shy about entering towns. The day she arrived a big male had stared her down from just thirty feet away before loping off into the underbrush.

A wolf? Not likely, though she'd read reports of wolves filtering into Colorado along the Wyoming border.

Her imagination?

She got up and turned on all of the interior lights on her way to the front entry, then she switched on the porch light and looked out the peephole in the door.

Nothing. She made a cup of decaf tea and lingered awhile in the kitchen, listening. Whatever it was, the blazing lights in the cottage had probably scared it away.

On her way back to bed she left the lights on and double-checked all the windows and door locks. Her cell phone within close reach on the nightstand, she burrowed back under the pile of down comforters and fell into a fitful sleep.

And dreamed of bears and wolves and tall, dark men coming to her rescue who all bore a remarkable resemblance to Jack McCord.

At the insistent, harsh buzz of her alarm clock, Mei sat upright in bed and drowsily peered at the time. How could it be six-thirty already? She'd planned to get to school early to grade papers and set up some experiments.

She leaped out of bed, showered and dressed at lightning speed and grabbed a yogurt and a banana on her way out the door into the early-morning gloom.

Her snow boot caught on a huge, furry object sprawled across the porch as she stepped outside and she went flying, the contents of her purse and her impromptu breakfast scattering across the porch.

She bit back a scream as she scrambled to her feet and backed away, not taking her eyes off—whatever it was. It stirred, then lumbered to its feet. Her heart sank as it rose to its full height—approximately that of a good-size pony—then slowly turned to face her. Its lips pulled back, revealing a heart-stopping array of sharp teeth.

If it was a predator, she was in deep, deep trouble.

Dropping her gaze briefly to the porch floor, she searched frantically for her car keys. Mei slowly reached down to grab them, then she warily backed all the way to the SUV she'd parked a few yards from the porch steps and threw herself inside, her heart hammering.

It was only when she got the door shut that she dared take a longer look at the creature, and she realized that her shock and fear had multiplied its size. It wasn't some massive mutant wolf or grizzly. Its tail was wagging weakly and that impressive armory of teeth was bared in a doggy grin, not a snarl. Underneath the grayish brown matted and shaggy coat, it was rail thin. Some sort of Newfoundland mix, maybe.

But it was the expression in its eyes that drew her slowly out of her vehicle. Fading hope. Hunger. Heartbreaking acceptance of the fact that it would find no rescuer here or anywhere else.

Standing in the lee of her open door for safety, she reached into her car for the plastic bag holding the half peanut butter sandwich she hadn't finished yesterday. "You hungry?" she murmured as she took the sandwich out of the bag and tossed it onto the porch.

The dog flinched and jumped backward, its tail between its legs and eyes filled with fear.

"It's okay, buddy," she crooned. "Eat it."

The dog crouched low, still cowering, its body shaking.

"Go ahead."

It watched her cautiously for several moments, then slunk forward and hesitated a few feet away from the food.

"It's all right, you poor thing. Eat it."

The dog moved closer, then wolfed it down. Then it backed up again and sat down to watch her, its tail waving back and forth against the porch floor.

Did it belong to someone? If so, it had been badly neglected or had been lost for a long while. It seemed to have no collar or tags and had clearly been malnourished for some time.

"I don't have dog food, buddy, but I'll pick some up. If you're still here when I get back, you've got yourself a meal."

She should call the sheriff's office. Check to see if there was still a dog pound somewhere in the county and have someone pick this stray up. But what then?

Maybe he wasn't actually grizzly size, but this was one massive dog and hardly a fluffy little house pet. She had no illusions about its fate unless there were no-kill shelters in the area.

The dog regarded her with such a sorrowful expression that her heart melted. "I'm going to the grocery store," she called out, hoping it at least would understand the welcoming tone in her voice. "You stay here and I will be right back."

"What on earth have you done?" Lisette demanded. "This creature is the size of a moose."

How her mom had picked up on the presence of Mei's new best friend so quickly proved that a mother's radar never waned. She'd marched down the lane just minutes after Mei arrived back home with a big bag of dog chow.

"What a good name for him. I was just heading for school, and found him on my porch. Homeless. Hungry. Isn't he sweet? Moose—I like that."

The dog finished off a bowl of kibble, then sat back on

its haunches and stared longingly at the bag of dog food leaning against the porch rail.

"Sorry, buddy," Mei said softly. "We'd better take it slow for starters."

"You certainly cannot have a dog like that here." Lisette stared at the dog with an expression of distaste. "It eats like a horse. It's surely loaded with fleas and germs and who knows what else. You work full-time so you aren't around. And my cottages are strictly posted as No Pets Allowed."

"I'm your *daughter*, Mom. And Moose isn't inside."

Yet.

"You have no idea whether he's even safe. He could attack other people. He could bite you. He could destroy... all sorts of things. And he's *filthy*."

"I'll try to find out if he has an owner. If he doesn't, I'll take him to the vet for shots and a bath."

Lisette held her little dog closer to her chest. "He could attack Albert and kill him with a single bite."

Moose looked up at Albert and wagged his tail vigorously. In turn, Albert struggled vigorously to escape her arms.

"I think they want to play, Mom."

"And I think that beast wants a second course. Hang on to him if you can. I'm taking Albert home." Lisette pivoted and strode toward her house but stopped a few feet away. "I want that dangerous animal gone. I'm calling the sheriff's office the minute I get back to my house. Surely they know of a dog pound that can deal with it."

Mei had no doubt that she was as good as her word.

Mom had always said that their house cats had simply run away, but more than one had disappeared after a single unfortunate incident in the house involving draperies or houseplants.

Moose looked up at Mei with sad eyes, his tail no longer wagging, as if he'd understood every word and had been down that road too many times before.

"I'm not letting it happen, buddy," she whispered. She pulled her cell phone out of her pocket and punched in 411 for information. "Let's see if we can find you a safe place across the creek until I get home from school."

Chapter Ten

Mei visibly sighed with relief when Jack appeared at the cottage fifteen minutes later. "I'm so thankful that you got my message. I have to leave for school in a few minutes, but I don't dare leave Moose here."

He stepped out of his SUV and met her on the front porch of her cottage, where Moose was curled up with his head and front paws on a fluffy pink bathroom rug. Jack raised a brow when Moose moved to her side and emitted a low, warning bark at his approach.

"Guard dog, is he?"

"I have no idea." She rested a hand on the dog's head. "This is a friendly guy, buddy. *Nice* man."

Jack cracked a smile. "I'm glad you think so."

The dog regarded Jack with suspicion, then grudgingly flopped down to lay at Mei's feet.

"I think Moose has adopted me. My mother isn't happy about it, though. Like I said on the phone, she's already calling the authorities about picking him up, and I don't want that to happen." She gently rubbed Moose's ears. "I'd rather try to find his owners myself, or find him a good home if need be. But I don't think he'll be safe here while I'm gone today."

"What is he? Half grizzly?"

"I have no idea about that, either. I'll see if I can get an appointment with the vet to check him out Saturday morning. Maybe she'll know."

He went back to his vehicle. "I brought an old collar and cable tie in my backseat left over from Fred's black lab. If he'll let you collar him, I'll keep him over at my place as long as you want."

"Thanks so much." She gratefully accepted the collar and sweet-talked to the dog as she fastened it around his neck. "If you take the dog food to your car, I bet he'll follow you right inside. I promise I'll come and get him after school."

Until yesterday Mei had always seemed aloof, reserved. A lofty, fragile princess who had rarely deigned to speak back in their high school days. Hearing her talk of her anguish last night and seeing her concern for this ragged dog revealed a side of her that he had never expected. Soft and sweet. Tenderhearted.

Once he had Moose stuffed in the backseat of his vehicle, he turned to her. "I can do some calling while you're in school. There must be some animal shelters around, and I can ask Zach if he knows of anyone missing a dog."

"Thanks." She rested a hand on his forearm. "I'll work on flyers to post around town. This is a wonderful favor, and I owe you one."

"Have dinner with me sometime. Or even just coffee."

Her eyes widened and then she dropped her gaze and took a small step back. "Maybe coffee sometime. When things quiet down a little."

"Sometime" sounded like a tactful version of "*don't hold your breath.*" He felt a flash of disappointment.

"No problem," he said mildly as he slid behind the

wheel and started the engine. "We're just neighbors, after all."

In the confines of the SUV, with its heater on, the odor of unwashed dog rapidly filled the compartment. Moose awkwardly scrambled into a different position, and when Jack looked back he found the dog trying to sit up on the seat, head lowered, shoulders jammed against the roof and three of its four paws on the floor. Moose wore a decidedly apologetic expression on his soulful face.

"You need a horse trailer, my friend."

"Aroooo—ooo."

He laughed at the dog's attempt to yodel a response. "And you need a bath. And maybe some breath mints."

The lane twisted around Lisette Clayton's home, and as he passed he glanced up at it, wondering what Mei's young life had been like in that house.

The curtains were open at one of the large plate-glass picture windows along the side. Like an angry sentinel, Lisette stood there glaring out at him, her arms folded across her chest, watching him leave.

He was all of twenty-nine, and yet the woman *still* had the power to make him shudder. There was no doubt in his mind that she would be confronting Mei shortly, to address the kind of company her daughter was keeping.

Come to think of it, it really didn't take much thought to guess at what kind of childhood Mei had experienced in that house while growing up.

Sadly, it took no imagination at all.

After an afternoon of watching the clock at school, Mei drove straight to Jack's place hoping Moose hadn't long since worn out his welcome and ended up in dog jail, after all.

When Jack didn't answer her knock on the residence

cabin door, she went over to the office and knocked, then tried the handle.

Locked.

Worry nipped at her heart as she shaded her eyes with her hand against the late-afternoon sun and surveyed the property. Neither the dog nor the man were anywhere to be seen. What if…

At the sound of a motor, she turned and saw Jack's SUV bouncing up the lane. He pulled to a stop on the other side of her vehicle and came around her front bumper.

"Sorry I didn't make it back before you got here," he called out, his dimples bracketing his mouth as he grinned. "Errands."

She bit her lower lip and again scanned the property. "My mom didn't send the dog catcher over here, did she?"

"If she did, Moose and I weren't here to greet him."

Relief flooded through her. "Whew. I was worried."

"I promised I'd babysit, and that's what I did. Sort of. Though I ended up needing a little help."

Jack's low laugh did funny things to her insides and suddenly she felt a flash of shyness. "Thanks, Jack."

"I…started a reclamation project but discovered I was way over my head."

He disappeared. A door opened and slammed shut. And then Jack strode toward her with a pony-size creature with a nimbus of white fur poofing out in all directions and a jaunty purple bow on its collar. "I found a dog groomer having a slow day."

She stared, her mouth dropping open in shock. "That's not Moose."

"That's what he'd like you to think. I believe he's embarrassed because the groomer didn't have any camo-green bows."

"I thought he was dark gray and tan."

"Dirt."

"I thought he was thin."

"He definitely is, under about sixty pounds of fluff." A corner of Jack's mouth lifted in a wry grin. "I was given specific orders never to bring him back in that condition again."

That Jack had even thought of doing this touched her heart. "I...I don't know what to say."

"Well, whatever you do, don't embarrass him. I made the mistake of laughing when I first saw him, and he still won't look me in the eye."

Sure enough, Moose had his head canted away from Jack and now that they were closer, Mei could see that his tail was between his legs.

"What a beautiful dog you are," she said, filling her voice with enthusiasm as she gave Moose's shaggy neck a hug. "You smell sooo good! And you are so, so handsome."

"How about me?" Jack teased.

"You're not nearly as fluffy as Moose here," she murmured as she cradled the dog's massive head in her hands and rubbed behind his ears.

Jack laughed. "Thank goodness."

She straightened. "This was the nicest thing anyone could've done for me, Jack. You not only saved him from my mother, but you gave him a spa day. He won't look nearly as scary to her now. What do I owe you?"

His eyes twinkling, he handed her the leash. "Consider it my gift to Moose, in recognition of his new life. If you hadn't taken him in, he might've gotten hit on the highway. Or if he'd had to start hunting for food, some farmer might've shot him."

"I can't let you pay for this, though. Just the gift of your time was really special." She impetuously hugged him, then awkwardly took a step back. "I'll bring a check over—or give it to you at church."

"You don't need to."

"Yes, I do. I can't tell you how much I appreciate what you've done. You're one special guy, no matter what—" Heat rushed to her cheeks as she faltered to a stop and resisted the urge to clap a hand over her mouth.

His mouth twitched. "No matter what anyone says?"

"What an awful thing to say," she moaned. "You've been nothing but kind to me, and then I blurt out something like that. I really, *really* need to stay away from some of my more vocal relatives…or learn to shut myself up."

"It's okay. Believe me, opinions run pretty strong on both sides. I can't say I'm very proud of the things certain people have done, but there's nothing I can do about it."

Moose sat at her side and bumped her hand with his head. She stroked his velvety ears. "So why did you come back here? You went to college out of state. You could have stayed there or could've gone anywhere in the world. Why return to a place where feelings run so high?"

"Cade."

"Of course. I'm sure you must've missed him."

A muscle ticked at the side of Jack's jaw. "He needed me. He needed a male role model and guidance because he sure wasn't getting much of either. But I guess I didn't quite succeed."

"He's a fine kid. Responsible, smart. Kind. You can be proud of him."

"Proud of him, yes. Happy with what he's doing, no. But Cade isn't going to change his mind, so like everyone else, I guess I've just got to step back and let the wedding proceed. Even if I've failed to protect him from a big mistake."

"Well, whether it is or not, he'll remember that you

loved him enough to try to help him. And since he's of legal age, you can't do much more than that."

Curled up in front of the fire, Moose unfolded himself into a long stretch, groaned with pleasure, then fell back asleep, the picture of contentment. Mei paused over a stack of exams she was grading to watch him fondly and stared into the flickering embers in her fireplace.

Life was so easy if one was a dog. Food, shelter, a nice warm fire, and life was good. Why was it so complicated for people? Everyone was so wrong about Jack. They continued their assumptions without ever pausing to really look at the man himself. A man with a kind heart who had moved back to a place where he wasn't welcome to help his brother. A thoughtful man who had taken time out of his day to help a bedraggled dog. A man who had graduated from college and who had a good job, yet was still being tarred with the same brush as Samuel Clayton's side of the family.

And where was the justice in that?

Life would be so much simpler if everyone just got along and quit reliving the past. Set aside old grievances. Maybe she couldn't change anyone else, but she was done standing by in silence when people were just flat wrong about each other—especially when it came to Jack McCord.

Mei tugged harder on the leash. Moose sat down, his tail limp and his sorrowful eyes filled with regret.

He was the most expressive dog she'd ever met and he'd charmed her completely, but the door to the vet clinic was still twenty feet away and the clock was ticking. "Please, Moose. Pretty please?"

A pickup slowed, then pulled up at the curb behind her

SUV. Vivienne climbed out and shaded her eyes against the late-afternoon sun. "Mei?"

Mei pleaded and tugged to no avail. "Yep—it's me."

"What do you have there, a wildebeest?"

"A stray. He…um…moved in the other day, and I want the vet to check him out. I named him Moose."

Vivienne strode up the sidewalk, skirting the icy spots, and wrapped her coat tighter around her slim waist. "Nothing ever grew that big without an owner to feed it, honey. Maybe you shouldn't invest too much money. Someone might want him back."

"Jack called the sheriff's department and the humane shelters in this part of the county. No one has reported anything like him."

Vivienne laughed. "I'm sure there isn't another one like him. Anywhere. Maybe he got loose just last night, and the owners haven't reported him yet." She paused. "You said *Jack?*"

"Jack McCord."

Vivienne's mouth fell open. "How on earth did Cade's brother get involved in all this?"

"As a favor. He was nice about it, too."

"Oh, my," Vivienne said faintly. "What did your mother say about that?"

"It doesn't matter." Though it would, once Mei finally got home tonight. Lisette would undoubtedly be marching right over to the cottage and have a lot to say.

Mei tried getting behind Moose and pushing. He immediately flopped down on the sidewalk as flat as a felled buffalo, a good 150 pounds of dead weight.

"I'd be careful if I were you. Jack was a troublemaker back in high school—one of Vincent's posse. I remember when…" Vivienne's voice trailed off. "Do you need some help, here?"

"I'd love it," Mei said through clenched teeth as she gripped Moose's collar and tried to haul him back to his feet. "If you'll pull, I'll push. I think he already knows this is a vet clinic and wants no part of it."

After another few minutes Moose finally gave in, lumbered to a sitting position and let Vivienne drag him through the front door with Mei pushing him from behind.

Vivienne waited while Mei checked in with the receptionist, then joined her at the back of the waiting room, where Moose tried to hide under a row of chairs and lifted several off the floor.

She waggled one eyebrow. "So tell me more about Jack."

"Nothing to tell. He took the dog to his place this morning and babysat it all day so Mom wouldn't send it off to dog jail while I was at school. He even took Moose to a groomer and refused to let me pay him back for it."

"What on earth possessed you to call Jack of all people?"

"He's a guest lecturer in one of my classes at the high school this month." Mei reined in a flicker of irritation at Vivienne's attitude. "He lives just across the creek from me, and he was an acquaintance in high school. Honestly, he's not one of the bad guys. He's really good with the students."

"Hmmmm."

"What's wrong with that?"

"Just be cautious," Vivienne said. "He's one very good-looking man, and he's mighty protective of his little brother, but he still associates with the wrong people in this town—people who very much want to see our side of the family lose Grandpa's inheritance."

"I wouldn't know about that. Like I said…he seems like a really nice guy."

"What if he's been kind only to gain the kind of information they can use to hurt you?"

Mei stared at her. "How can you say that? Look at Cade. He's a good kid, no matter what part of the gene pool he came from. And Jack isn't related to the Claytons at *all*. He's nothing like Charley or Vincent or all the others. I'm sure of it."

"So you think." Vivienne loosened her winter coat. "There's good reason that we grew up wary of Great-uncle Samuel and his progeny."

"Not all of them are like him."

"Most and especially Vincent. I can't even count all the nasty things he tried to pull over the years—"

A chair wobbled and tipped over with a crash and Moose leaped to his feet in panic, sending two others flying. Mei shot an apologetic glance at the receptionist as she straightened them all out.

When Mei took her seat again, Moose crowded next to her knees, trembling and staring at the other chairs as if they just might attack him again.

"Then again, I guess Cade turned out to be an upstanding young guy," Vivienne admitted. "Maybe a few of them aren't as bad as we think."

"If Jasmine has anything to do with it, there'll be even less conflict in the future. Do you think she can really pull off that Thanksgiving dinner and convince everyone to get along peacefully?"

"For a couple hours, maybe—as long as they're all busy eating." Vivienne shrugged. "But after that I think all bets are off...even when the turkey coma sets in. For some of them there's just been too much animosity over the years to let it go easily."

"And then there's the fact that Vincent isn't going to stop being Vincent."

"Sad, isn't it? If it wasn't for that clause in Grandpa George's will, maybe we could all work at making things better during the coming year. But now they have unbelievable motivation to cause trouble. And you can be sure they will."

Mei nodded. If Great-uncle Samuel's side of the family managed to drive away just one of Mei's cousins before the year was up, Samuel would inherit every last penny, every last acre of land. And eventually his greedy relatives would inherit it all from him.

Why had Grandpa put his beloved wealth at such risk? He and Samuel had never gotten along.

A slender blonde in a lab coat appeared by the receptionist's desk. "This must be Moose. Would you like to come on back?"

This time Moose trudged after her, his head and tail drooping, as if he knew he was heading for the gallows and had no more chances to escape.

"I've got to get back out to the ranch, hon." Vivienne waved them off. "Good luck with your beast."

Sunday morning dawned with six inches of fresh snow and stiff winds keening out of the mountains that frosted Mei's cottage windows with lace and blew snowdrifts across the streets in town.

After letting Moose out to do his business, she put him back inside the cottage and drove over to pick up her mother for church.

The silence in the vehicle was deafening by the time they reached Clayton Christian Church and parked out front. Mei started to open her door, then settled back in her seat. "Is there anything you want to talk about, Mom?"

Lisette's chin lifted. "We don't want to be late."

"Mom?"

Lisette sighed. "I'm not happy about the dog, to begin with. I specifically told you that you couldn't keep it on my property. It has to go by Monday."

"Did you know that he's probably half wolfhound, half Great Pyrenees? The vet says he has the personality to make a wonderful pet."

"Be that as it may, he's still a very large and smelly dog. I don't want him on my property."

"The vet says he's probably around two or three years old and surprisingly healthy given his very low weight from the fact that he's been starving. He'll be taking monthly pills for fleas and heartworm." Mei grinned. "He smells like peaches, but I think he's embarrassed about it."

Lisette sighed.

"He's a good watchdog, Mom. He barks if someone comes to the door." Mei looked over at her. "I've never felt so safe living alone. I hope no one claims him, and if that happens, I'll start looking for another place to live."

"Oh, Mei—" Lisette's voice was laced with disappointment.

She plowed on. "I really do understand your reasons for not wanting him around. But he's such good company that I just can't turn him in at the shelter and risk that he might be put to sleep."

Lisette's jaw tensed. "We'd better get inside or we'll be late for the service. We can talk about him later, but there are other, far more important things to discuss, too. After church."

The snow-drifted roads had kept some of the more rural members at home, but there were still a lot of familiar faces to see when Mei walked into church behind her mother. Most of the local shopkeepers. Mark Arrington, the Clayton family's lawyer who had presided over the reading of Grandpa George's will. Several old high school classmates, who turned and smiled. She caught a glimpse of Brooke, who was lingering at the back, deep in conversation with an elderly woman.

Vivienne and her new fiancé, Cody, were already seated in a middle pew with Zach and Kylie, and a young, school-aged girl Mei didn't recognize. Behind them, Jasmine and Cade were seated next to Arabella and a tall, handsome man who was likely Arabella's fiancé, Dr. Jonathan Turner.

Mei smiled to herself when she spied Arabella's triplets seated alternately between the adults, probably in hopes that the four-year-old girls would make it through the service in relative peace. They were such darling little things at that age, with their silky dark hair and big golden-brown eyes, just like their mother's, and Mei felt a pang in her heart at all she'd missed by not living here in Clayton. She'd seen the girls for the first time in July, and they were growing up way too fast.

Lisette took her customary seat in the fourth pew from the back, left side, and Mei slid in next to her. The scents of furniture polish and candles and of the old church itself swirled around Mei, enveloping her in memories from the distant past.

She thought back to the days when she and Lucas had been small and had sat in this very church between their parents, trying to keep still during the long sermons, and the cycle of life through baptisms and weddings and funerals. Mei had been so eager to leave for college and the chance to get away that she'd never looked back at what she was missing.

Maybe she'd never really belonged with her adoptive family or in this town of ranchers. She'd always looked different. Felt different. But Clayton was also the one town where everyone had once known her name and she'd known theirs—a world away from the anonymity she'd once gladly embraced in Denver and San Francisco.

"Howdy," a deep voice whispered. "Do you mind? Cade's pew is full."

Startled, she discovered Jack had slid in next to her. A little shiver coursed through her, and suddenly the beautiful stained-glass windows seemed brighter, the day filled with more promise. "No, of course not."

He leaned close. "How's Moose doing? Had any phone calls on him?"

"No calls, and he's doing fine. He even seems to be housebroken—though I'm still hoping for the best in that regard." She reached down to her purse on the floor, withdrew the check she'd written out earlier and handed it to him. "This is for making him beautiful. I just hope it's enough. I didn't know which groomer you went to, so I guessed."

"I don't want your money, Mei."

She tried to hold back a smile, but it wobbled free anyhow. "And I'm not taking it back."

Across the aisle, Mei saw Samuel peer at her and scowl, then turn to Charley and Pauley, who were seated next to him. A few rows in front of them, Arabella glanced over her shoulder at Jack, then fixed Mei with a dark look. And on Mei's other side, Lisette sniffed and radiated displeasure as she moved a few inches farther down, her posture as rigid as the hard, wooden pews. What was with these people?

Jack settled his hand over hers. "Maybe I shouldn't have joined you. Sorry."

"Don't be. You're a friend, and you have every right to sit anywhere you please. It's church. And if anyone calls me on it, they're going to find out exactly what I think."

He gave her hand a gentle squeeze, then released it. "My thoughts exactly."

The rustles and whispers in the church silenced as the organist began to play "How Great Thou Art" and the last few people trailed in. Reverend West took his place at the pulpit.

Mei settled back in the pew as the beautiful notes swirled around her.

She'd dreaded coming back to her hometown. Twelve long months here had seemed impossible. But now, as she surveyed the beautiful old church and sat among her friends and relatives who had gathered to worship, she felt a sense of peace fill her heart.

"Let's go downstairs to the fellowship hall for coffee," Mei whispered to her mother as they walked down the center aisle after the service.

Lisette shook her head. "I'd rather leave."

"I haven't talked to Arabella and her girls yet or met her fiancé. And I think I just caught a glimpse of Brooke on the other side."

"You could certainly talk to your cousins another time."

"Please?"

Lisette rested her fingertips on the white leather cover of her Bible as if she were searching for strength. "It's because of that...that Clayton."

"Jack? No—look, he's already talking to someone else. But he's Jack *McCord*, Mom. Not Clayton. And I'm sure you won't have to worry about him coming up to talk to us."

He'd already caught Mei's eye and silently canted his head toward her mother, so she knew that he'd stay well clear of Lisette to avoid any awkward encounters.

Lisette sighed. "Very well. But just a few minutes."

Mei cradled a cup of cocoa in her hands, savoring the warmth. The wind outside rattled the windows of the church fellowship hall and now and then a gust of snow slammed against its white clapboard siding. "Just listening to that wind makes me feel cold."

Arabella laughed. "You've been away too long. This is a balmy day. Just wait until January."

"Oh, I remember. I had to make that four-block trek on foot to and from high school often enough."

"Have you met my fiancé?" Arabella held out her hand and the tall, dark blond–haired man who had sat with her in church broke away from talking to Jack and Zach and sauntered over. "This is Jonathan Turner."

Mei offered her hand. "Nice to meet you, Jonathan. I hear you're starting up a new medical clinic here and that you even do house calls."

"That word got out a little too fast." He grinned and looped an arm around Arabella's shoulders to draw her closer to his side. "I'm already practicing here, though the clinic itself won't be done for a few more months."

He suddenly looked around, then he and Arabella looked at each other. "Where's Jessie?" they both said at once.

"Oh, dear. Excuse us—she's probably upstairs hiding under the altar again with a double handful of cookies. Can you keep an eye on Jamie and Julie for just a second? The girls all need to get to their Sunday School class."

Arabella and Jonathan hurried away, and Mei moved over to the long table where the other two little girls were eyeing the platters of cookies, punch and coffee. Today all three were dressed in pink frothy dresses with white tights and a big pink bow in their dark ringlets.

She fixed her gaze midway between the two. "Are you Jamie?"

One of the little girls nodded. "Who are you?"

"I'm Mei, your mom's cousin."

Jamie frowned. "You don't look like my mom."

Knowing that the topic of foreign adoptions would be way beyond her understanding, Mei just smiled. "I'm from far away. Can you tell me which cookies are the very best?"

The other child, who had to be Julie, pointed at cookies with M&Ms in them. "Those gots candy."

"It's good to see you again, Mei."

Mei turned and found her cousin Brooke smiling at her.

Mei started to offer her hand, then switched to an awkward hug. "Congratulations! I hear you're engaged."

Brooke beamed. "I am. Gabe and his little boy aren't here because A.J. is just getting over a bad cold, but I can't wait for you to meet him."

A chubby sad-eyed girl of nine or ten with long blond hair sidled up to Brooke, her expression downcast.

"This is Macy Perry," Brooke said. "She's a very special friend of mine. Macy, this is my cousin Mei. She's been on lots of adventures. She's lived in Denver and San Francisco, and way over in China."

The girl looked up at Mei and forced a smile, a single dimple flashing in her left cheek.

Mei stared down at her, momentarily stunned into silence as a brief memory flashed through her thoughts.

The family picnic out at the state park when Mei was fourteen and Brooke was nine. Mei had just overheard Grandpa George talking to her father, and he'd referred to her as "that little Asian girl of yours."

She'd listened in shock, her heart wrenching at the realization that her grandfather didn't think of her as anything but an outsider. Tears spilling down her cheeks, she'd wandered far from the group to sit at the edge of the lake, feeling more alone than ever, when little Brooke bounced up to her and chattered gaily about her new puppy.

Brooke, with her sweet disposition and sunny smile, had somehow known what Mei needed at that moment. Glancing at Macy again, Mei suddenly realized that the young girl looked almost exactly like Brooke had at that age. Right down to that single dimple.

Mei floundered for something to day. "Um…it's…it's really nice to meet you, Macy. Have you lived around here long?"

"Always." The girl shot a questioning look up at Brooke, then added, "My mama is really sick, so she isn't here."

"I'm sorry to hear that, honey."

"She's coming to my house to bake cookies today." Brooke circled an arm around Macy's shoulders to give her a quick hug but gave Mei a speaking look over the girl's head. "I love it when she can visit me."

Something wasn't quite right here.

When Macy wandered away toward the triplets, Brooke drew Mei into a quiet corner of the room. "Macy's mother is terminally ill. Just in the past week or so she's taken a precipitous turn for the worst. Hospice is involved, and they say Darlene could go anytime in the next month or two."

"Oh, no." Mei glanced over at the child, her heart wrenching for all poor Macy was going through.

"Gabe and I promised her mother that Macy can live with us, but all of us on the Church Care Committee have been involved—helping Darlene, taking in Macy on her mother's worst days. I dread these last weeks for Macy's sake."

"What about her father? Is he in the picture?"

"Darlene refuses to tell us who he is, which is strange because she's deeply worried about her daughter's future. Wouldn't you think she'd want us to tell him about the situation?"

Mei sighed. "She wouldn't if he was a terrible person. Drugs, alcohol abuse. You never know."

Again the image of Brooke as a young girl flashed through Mei's thoughts. "Is...is Macy a relative?"

"No. Why?" A defensive edge crept into Brooke's voice. "She doesn't need to be. We would help anyone in this awful situation, relative or not."

"I didn't mean it the wrong way. It's just a coincidence, I guess, but she sort of reminds me of you when you were young."

Brooke's expression softened. "Thanks. Macy is a sweet girl."

Lisette appeared at Mei's side. "It's time to go, dear. People are leaving and I have things to do at home."

"Hi, Lisette. It's nice to see you here." Brooke's eyebrows rose. "Whoa. I have a *wonderful* idea. One of the committees here at church has lost a few members lately, and we could really use more help. Both of you would be *perfect.*"

Lisette stiffened. "I don't think—"

"It's easy," Brooke exclaimed. "And there's such a need. We visit shut-ins and run errands for those who can't get out. Babysit for our single parents who need a break or for those caring for a spouse with Alzheimer's. Because there's no taxi service here, we help our older members get to their doctor and dentist appointments. Some of us make meals for people who've just been discharged from the hospital."

"I'm sorry, I just don't think I'm up to that." Lisette

rested a firm hand on Mei's arm. "And right now, I think I'm developing a migraine. I really do need to go home."

Brooke lowered her voice. "Starting a week ago, we've been taking turns at staying with Darlene in shifts around the clock at her apartment because she's so weak now. I was thinking maybe—"

Lisette shook her head. "No. Mei, you can do whatever you wish, but I have no experience with such illness. No medical training whatsoever. And I will not place that woman or anyone else at risk because of my limitations."

"Neither of you would have to help us with Darlene's care, but there are other ways you could help us tend to others in need. Please? Even for a little while?" Brooke grinned. "I know I'm being a shameless beggar, but it would help so much now that we're shorthanded."

During her trip here from San Francisco, Mei had been mulling over ways she could try to get her mother involved in the community before she ended up a bitter and lonely recluse, and this would be ideal.

"We would love to help, Brooke. Sign us up."

"Mei!" Lisette said.

"It's perfect, Mom. We can even participate as a mother-daughter team, and it will be such fun."

"I can't. I just—"

"Yes, you can. It's a small community. It won't take a lot of effort, and I think it's time for both of us to help out in some way. Don't you?"

"Jack."

At the sound of the gruff, familiar voice, Jack turned around slowly. Samuel may have been his temporary grandfather for the few years Jack's mother was married to Charley, but they'd never been close. "Good morning."

With his bushy gray eyebrows, deeply lined face set in

a permanent scowl and the burly build of someone who'd been a fierce pro wrestler in his day, he could be an intimidating man.

But it was his shifty gaze that revealed more about him than anything else.

"So," Samuel growled, "you still haven't done anything about that brother of yours."

Jack instantly bristled. "Excuse me?"

"The fool kid is making a *major* mistake."

Jack might inwardly agree, but faced with Samuel's harsh words he found himself recoiling. "There's nothing anyone can do to prevent it," he said evenly. "But I'm not sure what difference it will make to your family."

"He's a traitor. And now that silly girl of his thinks we're all supposed to come to some dinner at Thanksgiving and play nice. Cade told me about it yesterday. She can just go on thinking everyone is coming if she wants to, but it ain't gonna happen."

"That's certainly your choice," Jack retorted. "Though I expect the people who attend will think you were afraid to show up."

"Afraid of what?"

He shrugged. "You tell me, I guess."

"And what's this I see right here in church? You're getting awfully friendly with Lisette and that daughter of hers. Neither one of 'em are worth the time of day, far as I'm concerned—just a rich widow and her spoiled brat."

Jack tried to keep his temper in check. "That's not fair at all."

"Fair? Vern and Lisette Clayton were the snootiest, most self-righteous people I ever met, and that girl of theirs sure followed suit. She didn't lower herself to talk to anyone around here when she was growing up." Samuel's voice dripped sarcasm. "Must've thought she was mighty special, being the doctor's daughter."

"She was shy. Painfully shy. And if people around here had been more kind and accepting, it would have helped her a great deal."

Samuel's face turned an ugly red. "Just you keep thinking over your choices around here. Choose the wrong side, and life can end up a lot tougher than you can imagine."

Revulsion crawled through Jack. "I hope that wasn't a threat."

"Threat? Just the honest truth. You got me and the boys at your back and you always did. You owe us for that—and all we done for you. So don't forget it."

Chapter Eleven

By the time Mei drove into her mother's driveway, Lisette had leaned her head against the headrest, her eyes closed and fine lines of tension bracketing her eyes. "We're home, Mom. Can I help you with anything, or do you just want to go in and take a nap?"

"You've helped quite enough already," she snapped. "I just need my pain medication and to be left totally alone for the rest of the day. And after that, you and I need to have a talk."

She eased slowly out of the SUV and moved to her front door as if she were walking on eggshells to avoid jostling the pounding drums in her head.

Mei felt a sliver of guilt as she watched her mother slowly unlock the door and disappear inside. *I shouldn't have been so pushy,* she muttered to herself as she drove the rest of the way to her cottage and let herself in.

Once again she'd inadvertently found a way to aggravate Mom, when all she'd wanted to do was help. It had been an ongoing cycle throughout her childhood—trying to do the right thing and never quite succeeding. At the age of twenty-eight, apparently she still couldn't get it right. When would she ever learn?

Moose met her inside the cottage with a happy woof and his madly waving flag of a tail, and her heart lifted. "At least you love me," she sang to him as she hugged his neck. "Let's go for a walk."

Lisette appeared at Mei's door at eight in the evening, looking drawn and haggard, her usually flawless makeup smudged and her hair mussed.

Mei's mouth dropped open. "Oh, Mom—I'm so sorry about your headache. Are you all right? Should you even be out of bed?"

"I'm better. Can I come in?"

"Of course." Mei stepped aside to usher her in, then took her coat and hung it on the ceramic-tipped brass coat hooks by the door. "Coffee? Tea or cocoa?"

"Nothing, thank you. I'm just here to talk." She moved to the settee in the living area, eyeing Moose with distaste on the way. "So he's still here."

"I put out flyers, but I haven't had a single phone call about him. Isn't he sweet? He's been curled up in front of the fireplace all evening. And just think—now he's all silky and clean, and he doesn't have a single flea."

"I still pray that he will find a good home. Elsewhere. I don't want animals in my cottages, and I'm not happy about you going against my wishes. But—"

Mei couldn't contain her smile. "You'll let him stay? You won't be upset?"

"Those are two very different questions, Mei. But I don't think you can find another decent place to rent in this town. Even if you could, no *livable* place would allow you to have such a dog." Lisette sighed. "So, because I want you to be safe, he may stay."

"Thanks, Mom!" Mei surged forward to give her a hug, but Lisette held up a hand.

"This is contingent on his behavior. If he proves himself to be destructive, noisy or careless in his house manners, you must promise to get rid of him, with no further questions asked."

"Definitely." She went ahead and gave her a hug, though Lisette stiffened in response.

Mei dropped back to sit on the rocking chair facing the settee. "Is something else wrong?"

"What quality is most important in a relationship, do you think?"

"Trust. Honesty. Caring."

"Let's go with trust and honesty. Without them you have nothing to build on. No assurance of the future. They are more important than *anything* else."

"Okay, I'll agree with that."

Lisette flicked a hand impatiently. "Then why would you choose to associate with someone of poor character, from the disreputable side of the family, who once spread lies about your own brother and then denied doing so? That and the fact that you have chosen to be sneaky about seeing him just breaks my heart. Trust and honesty are everything, Mei. Between husbands and wives, parents and children."

Mei blinked. "Seeing him? I'm not sure what you mean."

"You know how our family feels about the likes of Vincent and Jack and all the rest. And yet, you didn't bother to tell me that Jack McCord is teaching in your classroom. Or that he now occupies the wildlife biologist's quarters on the other side of Silver Creek—and I know you've been over there at least twice." Lisette drew a sharp breath. "Worse, Maude Miller saw you meet him at the Cowboy Café and you were observed kissing the man on the street, for all the world to see."

Speechless, Mei flopped back in her chair.

"Well?" Lisette's voice turned to steel. "Tell me none of this is true."

"I barely knew him in high school, Mom. But he's a nice guy no matter what you think. It's true I asked him to help me with Moose. And I went over to check on him once to make sure he didn't get hurt during a bear counting expedition."

"So then you had to ask him to teach in your classroom? Was that really necessary?"

"The previous science teacher scheduled him as a speaker, and the kids are fortunate. He's a real asset in the class."

"She certainly didn't schedule your behavior on one of the busiest streets in town."

"That?" Mei reined in a crazy urge to laugh. "I stopped at the café when I saw Zach's patrol car and went in to ask him about the search for Lucas. He and Zach were together, and Jack expressed his sympathies afterward. He was offering comfort, not taking me on a hot date. You've got to trust me more than this, Mom."

Lisette glared at her. "Trust. Hard won and easily lost. You'd better remember that because I'm afraid you're going down the wrong path."

"Jack has no romantic interest in me. And don't worry… because even if there were a possibility between the two of us, there'd be no point. I'm heading back to San Francisco when my year is up—and nothing is going to change my mind."

Mei stood outside the environmental science classroom on Monday afternoon as the students filed into the room and she watched for Jack to arrive.

He'd been kind, he'd been thoughtful—willing to help

with Moose at a moment's notice. He'd certainly shown his compassion for her that evening outside the Cowboy Café.

But luckily, she hadn't seen him since church.

It was fortunate because now she knew that even the most innocuous meetings could spark gossip in this town, and setting off her mother's fragile nerves again was something she really wanted to avoid. She just hoped Jack would understand, though this wasn't the time nor the place to discuss it.

Sure enough, he showed up on time, wearing a heavy backpack and carrying several different coils of climbing rope on his shoulder. He also held a canvas bag with a screened window at one end.

"Thank you for coming," she said politely, holding the door open so he could walk in. She avoided meeting his gaze, but her pulse still fluttered when he walked up to her. "The kids are really looking forward to this."

He paused, waiting until she looked up at him, and gently closed the door instead. "Is something wrong?"

She glanced both ways down the empty hallway. "Nothing. Nothing at all. Are you all set for your lecture?"

"Definitely." He grinned and held up the bag. "I plan to discuss search and rescue and the world of wildlife biology. I even brought a friend. If it's one that slithers, will you mind?"

He *had* to be joking. "You brought a snake?"

His eyes twinkled. "A very gentle, quiet snake. Promise."

"Um…okay." But the contents of the bag seemed to be *moving*. She suppressed a shiver, remembering the day when Vincent dropped a large, writhing snake in her lap and laughed at her screams.

She forced a smile. "We need to get in there and get started before those kids go crazy."

"You seem upset. I can take Sid back out to my truck."

"No. Really, it's fine."

He eyed her thoughtfully. "If you're on edge because of that dinner invitation, I promise not to put you on the spot again. I know it must have been a frightening prospect."

"Not really. It's just…awkward."

"Maybe you could agree to dinner sometime and get it over with. It couldn't be as bad as, say, a root canal. At least from what I've heard."

She tried to hold her mouth in a stern line, but it twitched, and that gave him a glimmer of hope. "It isn't as simple as you think, Jack."

"I know that. I got a lecture from Samuel after church."

"You did?" Her eyes widened, and then she laughed. "We should compare notes because I got one from my mother, too. Isn't it ridiculous? I'm twenty-eight and you're a year older, but we're *still* getting advice."

Samuel's "advice" had been couched in a veiled threat, but Jack just nodded. "Maybe it's time we ignore them all."

"I'm serious. Please, let's go in before my class takes the room apart."

He wasn't backing down. "Then we can talk afterward?"

"Yes…no…" She threw up her hands in frustration. "We'll see. A few minutes maybe."

He walked into class and set his canvas bag on the desk in front. "How many of you have started your research on endangered species in Colorado?"

Just a few students raised their hands.

"You need to choose the species that you want to research on our field trip. I believe Ms. Clayton will post the sign-up sheet tomorrow."

Mei nodded when he looked her way.

"Good. So who can tell me about the Clayton County Search-and-Rescue Team?"

No one responded.

"We're a countywide, all-volunteer nonprofit organization, with around fifty members. But that doesn't mean just anyone can walk off the street and jump right in. Our minimum age for the rescue team is twenty-one, and each volunteer undergoes at least a year of training before he or she is allowed to take a written test and field test for participating with the team."

He glanced around the room. "What kind of volunteers do you think we need?"

A husky boy in the center of the room grinned and pointed to his chubby arms. "Guys with a lot of muscle, like me…or not."

Everyone laughed.

"We need strong, capable men and women, true. But we also need people to help with office duties and give presentations to student groups or to be on the backup crew. So keep the program in mind if you find yourself wanting to volunteer somewhere." He dropped his climbing ropes on a table, then emptied his backpack. "I brought in some rescue equipment so you could take a look."

Mei let her thoughts drift as Jack talked for twenty minutes about rescue missions, search-and-rescue statistics and the cost of maintaining the program, then segued into his life as a wildlife biologist.

Her mother's words kept coming back to her, and something about them just didn't seem right. What had touched such a raw nerve to upset her so much? If her anger still stemmed from Vincent's long-ago false accusations against Lucas, then her emotional reaction now was way out of proportion. She'd always been moody, but why would she hold such a grudge for so long?

At a collective gasp throughout the room followed by squeals of delight, she jerked her attention back to the present and found that Jack now held a golden-tan snake with a black checkerboard pattern on its back, and he was walking slowly up and down the aisles. "Anyone know what this is?"

One of the girls cowered back in her chair as he passed. "Rattler!"

Ricardo laughed and reached out to stroke the snake as Jack passed. "Nope, it's a bull snake."

"Exactly right. The color patterns may be a bit similar, but this one isn't poisonous. If you have one in your yard, you're actually very, very lucky. What do you think they eat?"

A dozen hands shot up.

"Mice?"

"Rats?"

"Other snakes?"

Jack smiled. "Good guesses. Some people kill them on sight, and that's such a tragedy, because these are good fellas to have around. They are harmless to people, and depending on the size of the snake, they eat vermin like rats, mice, gophers, prairie dogs and rabbits. They prefer warm-blooded prey, but some sources say they'll eat baby rattlers and help keep the population of rattlesnakes down. I haven't seen that myself, though."

Gina reached out to touch it, too. "I thought it would be slimy, but it's cool and dry, like leather."

"Exactly right, Gina. How many of you think you'd like to be an actor someday?" When several girls raised their hands, he grinned. "These guys are expert actors from birth. They have no venom. They aren't aggressive and much prefer fleeing from danger. But if cornered and seriously frightened, they will actually use their acting ability and try to scare away their enemies. They will inflate their heads into the triangular shape of a rattler's, coil, shake the end of their tail and strike."

Tina, the heavyset redhead in the back row, shuddered. "I'd be scared."

"Which is the whole point—it's a very successful defense mechanism. Unfortunately, that behavior convinces some people that the bull snake is a rattler, and too many of these helpful fellows are killed for no reason." Jack settled the snake back into the canvas bag, then handed out a stack of colorful flyers. "Keep these and show them to your family and friends. The photos compare the appearance of a bull snake to the rattlers indigenous to this area, and there's a list of all the reasons why bull snakes benefit us. Any questions?"

He fielded questions for the last ten minutes of class. "When I come again Wednesday, we'll talk about big predators in the Rockies and mountain safety and plan our field trip, which will be on Friday. We will be gone for half the day, in the afternoon, so let your other teachers know that you'll be gone—and don't forget your permission slips, or you won't be getting on the bus. Finally, if you have any questions, Ms. Clayton will be working with you on your research, your plans for gathering data while we're up in the mountains and your individual projects."

The bell rang, and the students all launched to their feet, jamming notebooks in backpacks. But unlike the last time Jack was here, only a few charged for the door. The rest surrounded him, peppering him with questions.

Mei watched, amused and even a little touched. His ready smile and the flash of his dimples charmed her. His patience and thoughtful, intelligent answers spoke to his character.

In the face of her mother's wrath yesterday, she'd resolved to keep her distance from Jack, just in the interest of peace. Upsetting Mom hadn't seemed worth the unexpected opportunity of a friendship with the object of her teenage fantasies. But every time she encountered him, Jack seemed to reveal new depths, and she felt drawn to him all the more.

The last of the students finally cleared the room.

"You're doing a wonderful job with this," Mei said as she straightened the surface of her desk and pulled her purse from the bottom drawer. "The kids love having you here."

"Thanks. I enjoy teaching, but knew I wouldn't be happy confined indoors nine months of the year. My job is the best of all worlds, I guess—I'm outside a lot but have opportunities like this in the community."

"Better be careful. At the rate you're going, I think every one of these students will be after your job in the future."

"That's cool." The corners of his eyes crinkled when he smiled. "I get the feeling I'm not doing a good job of impressing their teacher, though."

"Of course you are. Like I said, you're doing a great job with the class."

"How's your dog?"

"Fine. My mom actually relented last night. Unless he makes trouble, he can stay." She gave a rueful laugh. "Though she probably changed her mind because I'd said I would look for a different place to live if he couldn't stay, and it would reflect badly on her if I did."

"I got the feeling that she wasn't exactly pleased when I sat in your pew on Sunday."

"There's so much that I don't understand about her now that I'm an adult." Mei hesitated. "I'm really sorry if she hasn't exactly been friendly to you and your family."

"All of us have issues to work through now and then. Sometimes it takes a lot of work, time and prayer to get past all of that and move on."

"And sometimes it just doesn't happen." Mei fingered the strap of her purse, debating.

She'd come back to her hometown to satisfy Grandpa George's will, but she'd also wanted one more chance to become a close part of her adoptive family. To finally feel as if she finally, truly belonged. But her mother and most of her close relatives still viewed Jack as an unsavory jerk who had caused trouble with Vincent as a teenager and would likely do it again.

She'd already resolved to defend him and his brother if the subject came up with her relatives. She would not stand by and listen to the old gossip ever again without taking a stand. But did she dare risk openly flaunting her family's opinion by going one step further?

Her head said no, but her heart...

"I really would like to be friends, Jack," Mei said firmly. "I think my mom's attitude is wrong. Maybe I can't change it, but I don't have to follow in her footsteps, either."

His eyes twinkled. "Mei the rebel."

"The grown-up," she retorted with a smile. "One who would like very much to go for that cup of coffee."

Chapter Twelve

The Cowboy Café was just as busy after school now as it had been when she was in high school. Now that she'd been back in town awhile, she was starting to recognize faces again, though a lot of the people here were strangers.

A slender waitress with a long auburn ponytail ushered Mei and Jack to a table in back, then waited, pencil poised over her order tablet. "Hey, Jack. Good to see you. What can I get you two to drink?"

"Just coffee for me, black."

"Really?" She pulled an incredulous face. "There's still a slice of Arabella's lemon meringue pie in back, and it has your name on it."

He grinned at her. "Sold."

"I should hope so. And for you, miss?" She smiled expectantly at Mei, then did a double take. "Mei? Mei Clayton?"

The years fell away as Mei remembered her from school, though Erin had been three years younger. She'd matured into a beautiful young woman. "And you must be Erin Fields, right? It's great to see you."

"I never exactly dreamed of doing this, but dreams do change." Erin smiled. "I own the café now."

"That's wonderful. This must be the busiest place in the county."

"Some days it is, and for that I'm more than grateful. So what can I get you?"

"Just coffee. Cream and sugar."

Erin nodded, and moments later she was back with their order. She lingered for a moment, fidgeting with the worn class ring on her hand. "I'm so sorry to hear about your brother, Mei. Have you heard anything yet?"

Lucas was never far from her thoughts, and now a fresh surge of worry crawled through her. "Not a word. Zach says the police and a P.I. are trying to find him, but I just can't understand why it's taking so long."

Erin bit her lower lip. "There are a lot of people praying for him. We all hope to hear good news soon."

The waitress drifted away toward the lunch counter. Jack took a slow sip of coffee, then started on his truly monumental slice of lemon pie.

"They must really like you here," Mei teased.

"They do." The corners of his eyes crinkled. "Erin operates a horse rescue in her spare time. Some visitors left a gate unlocked a while back, and a half dozen horses turned up miles away. I helped catch the escapees out on the highway."

"Exciting day."

"It was—with semi horns blaring and the horses running back and forth across the asphalt. They sure stopped traffic for a while." He speared another bite of pie with his fork. "Erin said she was giving me free pie for life after that, but I always add the entire cost to my tip."

"You are quite a hero."

He winked at her. "If it involves Arabella's pie, I'll go to any lengths. Believe me."

A warm feeling came over Mei as she studied him

across the table. How could her family have been so wrong about a man like him?

"Did I hear my name?" Arabella eased sideways past two full tables of teenagers and paused at their seats. "Nice to see you both." She gave Jack and Mei a curious look. "Together."

"He says he loves your pie," Mei said. "Want to join us?"

"Can't. I'm just here delivering dinner rolls for the supper rush, and I need to get back home to the girls because Jasmine wants to spend the evening with Cade. Imagine that." She rested a hand on Mei's shoulder. "It was good to see you on Sunday, Mei. I'm so glad you and your mother agreed to join the Church Care Committee."

A swallow of coffee went down the wrong way, and Mei leaned forward, coughing. She dabbed at her eyes with the edge of her napkin. "About that—I'm not sure I should have spoken for my Mom. She seemed a little upset with me on the way home."

Arabella laughed. "You could've fooled me. I saw her and Maude Miller at the church an hour ago working on some food pantry baskets to take to our shut-ins."

Mei's mouth dropped open.

"It's true." Arabella's eyes danced. "Maude took me aside and said she stopped by your mom's place and took her by surprise. When it comes to Maude, people don't often know what hit them until they find themselves knee-deep in work at the church."

"Did…did my mom look upset when you saw her?"

"Actually, she'd already started giving other people orders about how to fill the deliveries. If I didn't know her better, I'd say she was having a great time."

"That's amazing."

"Oh, and speaking of that, we could really use you for

a couple hours tomorrow, Mei. One of the people on our schedule can't spend time with Macy Perry after school tomorrow, and we need someone from four until eight. Are you available?"

"Of course. No problem."

Arabella pulled a pen from her purse and wrote the directions on a napkin. "Here you go. It's outside of town but not hard to find."

After school the next day Mei read the directions Arabella had written on the back of a Cowboy Café napkin and followed them to a forlorn little farmhouse out in the country.

It stood alone, the barns and corral long gone, on a little rise surrounded by winter-bare trees. An old windmill with missing blades still stood at the back of the yard, creaking in the icy wind.

Still, the house had been painted not long ago, and the drive was freshly plowed. The work of the Church Care Committee, maybe?

She could see the bumper of an old Mercury parked in a crumbling shed. The only other vehicle in sight was a newer sedan parked by the back door of the house. Another one of the volunteers probably.

She drove in, parked by the shed and went to knock on the back door. When no one answered, she tried to peer through the window in the door. The house appeared dark inside, silent and foreboding, and despite its bright blue paint and white trim, it emanated a sense of hopelessness.

She heard soft footsteps inside and saw a young face bob upward to peer through the glass. There were muffled voices inside. Then the heavy storm door creaked open and Macy stood before her, her cheerful pink eyeglasses at odds with her pale face. Her blue eyes were dulled with sadness.

"You're Mei," she said flatly. "My mama says to come in."

Another person emerged from the gloom inside. Mei recognized her as one of the brunette, middle-aged women who had served at the church coffee hour last weekend.

"I'm Carla," she said in a quiet voice. "I'm so glad you could come today. Arabella said you were going to take Macy out for supper and then to your place. She'll like that." She rested a gentle hand on Macy's shoulder. "Won't you, honey? This is the lady who has a giant fluffy dog as big as an elk. Or so I've heard."

Macy nodded, her expression somber.

"Go get your things then, Macy." Carla waited until Macy disappeared into the house, then lowered her voice. "Arabella probably told you that between the volunteers and hospice, people are here around the clock now. Darlene has failed so much in the past week or two that no one knows how much longer she has."

"How awful for Macy."

"She's slipping into organ failure related to her end-stage lupus, and there's nothing more that can be done."

"I'm so, so sorry."

"Macy doesn't like to leave her mom, but we try to get her out for a while several times a week. Otherwise, we try to have someone here after school and on weekends to help her with homework, play games or just sit with her and talk. If…anything changes while you're gone, we have your cell number."

Macy appeared with a coat on and her backpack hooked on one shoulder. She looked up at Mei. "Mama wants to see you first. She doesn't like me going with anyone she doesn't know."

"It sounds like she's a very good mom, Macy. Can you take me to her?"

The child nodded and turned on her heel, then led the way through the kitchen to a small living room where a hospital bed was set up against a wall. A table at the head of the bed was filled with dozens of prescription bottles, packages of gauze and medical supplies that overflowed onto a coffee table.

The television mounted above the fireplace was turned on to a channel with cartoons, the colorful glow from the screen casting a garish watercolor effect across the darkened room. The sound was barely audible.

The room was clean, yet the odors of medicine and dressings and end-stage disease permeated the air, making it difficult to draw a deep breath.

Macy stepped aside, but her gaze was riveted on Mei, as if she were hovering and ready to protect her mother.

The woman in the bed might have melted away into the mattress for what little evidence there was of her body beneath the sheet and blankets. She raised a bony arm and motioned, then her arm dropped limply across the blankets.

She weakly rolled her head toward Mei, her thin auburn hair fanning across pillows. "You're one of the Clayton cousins?"

Her voice was so whisper-soft that Mei leaned over the rail to hear better over the alternating humming and puffing sounds from the oxygen compressor. "That's right. I've been teaching high school in San Francisco, but now I'm teaching here for the next year." She rested her hand lightly on Darlene's skeletal wrist and smiled. "I'm Vern and Lisette's daughter. Do you remember them?"

Darlene silently looked up at her, her breathing ragged.

"My brother is Lucas," Mei said, speaking louder. "My cousins are Brooke, Zach, Arabella and Vivienne."

"I…I know them. They've all…been so kind."

"I came out to take your daughter into town for supper, and then I thought she could come to my place for a while. We can work on her homework or she can play with my dog, and she and I can talk. Is that all right?"

Darlene's eyes, so large and vacant in her gaunt face, searched Mei's for a long moment. "It…it's good for her to get away. Thank…you."

Mei smiled down at her, her heart breaking. Despite the ravages of her disease she could see that Darlene had once been a lovely woman. And even though she appeared to have little time left in this world, she was still struggling to put her daughter first. How could life be so cruel, to take away a loving mother when her daughter was still so young?

"We'll be back in a few hours, so don't you worry a bit. She's in good hands, I promise."

Macy had barely spoken through her supper at the Cowboy Café and just picked at her cheeseburger, fries and strawberry malt, so the waitress fixed to-go containers and Mei brought them back to her cottage for later.

As soon as Macy walked in the door of the cottage, her face brightened and she stared at Moose in awe. "He's yours? He's really yours?"

"He sort of found me a while back," Mei said as she pulled a leash from the coat hooks by the door. "I need to take him outside for a few minutes. Do you want to eat your supper while it's still warm?"

Macy shook her head. "I want to come along. He's like…he's like a pony!"

"That was my first thought exactly."

They stepped back out in the darkness. The wind had finally calmed and the sky was clear, revealing a thick blanket of stars.

"Where I live now—or did, anyway—there are so many lights that you can barely see any stars," Mei said as they started down the lane. "I'd forgotten just how breathtaking this is."

Moose walked on one side, and Macy walked silently on the other, looking upward.

"My mama says I should name a star after her. Then I can always see her watching over me from up there, no matter what." Her voice broke. "Sh-she'll be in heaven, but I won't be able to see her there."

"How are you feeling about all of this, sweetheart? I know it must be very hard."

Macy batted at her cheeks with her mittens. "It isn't fair. I don't want her to be sick. I want her to be here with me."

Mei wrapped an arm around the girl's shoulders and gave her a comforting hug. "I know you do."

"But she says everyone has a time to die, and we don't get to choose. And she says she'll love me forever and ever, even if she can't live here anymore."

"Of course she will."

"But when I get old, I'll be in heaven with her, and it will be a wonderful time." A faraway look filled Macy's eyes. "She'll be there with the biggest hug in the whole world."

"She's a wonderful mom."

Macy sniffled and wiped at her face again. "I try to be brave and not cry. I don't want her to feel bad about leaving me 'cause she can't help it. But it's h-hard." Her voice grew more subdued. 'Specially 'cause I never had a dad. He died before I was born."

Mei's heart twisted over the suffering this poor, sweet girl was enduring. "But you'll always have all of us to love you forever and ever. And way back when she first got sick, your mom made sure that you'd have a wonderful home. Right?"

"With Brooke and Gabe." Macy's lower lip trembled. "They promised."

Relief flooded through Mei. Brooke was a sweetheart and would be a wonderful mom. With Brooke's upcoming marriage to Gabe, Macy also would gain a new daddy and a brother.

"Would you like to hold the leash?"

"Really?" Macy's eyes widened as she took another look at Moose. "What if he runs away?"

"Believe me, he doesn't seem to go anywhere very fast. I think his favorite speed is 'whoa.'"

Macy sputtered, then choked out a laugh—a rusty sound that surely had seen little use during all the time she'd sat by her dying mother.

Mei swooped down to give her a big hug, wishing she could take away all that sorrow, then she handed the leash over. "Here you go, Macy. You now hold the reins to the slowest pony Colorado has ever seen."

Chapter Thirteen

"Okay, kids," Jack called out to the environmental science students. "Remember what we talked about on Wednesday?"

The students milled impatiently around the campsite.

"Let's hear it, folks," he said, his voice louder.

"Outdoor safety."

"Bears."

"Mountain lions."

Gina affected a bored look, as usual. "Try not to disappear or get killed."

"Just to get our bearings again, the trail past the latrines takes you back to the school bus. It's just an easy quarter-mile down to the parking lot. There's a map in your packet, exactly like the one you see on the bulletin board at the head of each trail radiating from this point." His voice rang with authority as he addressed the students. "You are to stay within a hundred-yard radius of this campsite on any one of the three marked trails. You are to go no farther than the red flags I placed on each trail. Understood?"

"It's cold out here," Gina mumbled, jamming her mittened hands under her armpits. "This is stupid."

Mei gave her a quelling look. "It's thirty-four degrees

with bright sunshine, and the snow cover is only a few inches deep here. We'll be here just an hour, so I think you'll survive."

"My feet are cold!"

Mei looked down at the girl's heavy snow boots. "If you feel you can't handle it, you can go back and sit in the heated bus with the driver. I'll call Mrs. Chermak on the bus to let her know you're coming, and she'll keep an eye on anyone who chooses to go back."

Gina rolled her eyes. "Well, *that* would be fun. She treats us like we're in first grade."

With good cause, Mei thought to herself. "If you choose to go back, you have to check in with Mr. McCord or me. No exceptions. Now, does anyone have questions on how to record their data? Don't forget—this was purposely scheduled for November so you'd have a chance to study the winter environment and also have a chance to see tracks. Mr. McCord and I will circulate through the group in case there are any questions."

Notebooks held in the crooks of their arms and pens held in mittened grasps, the class fanned out, toeing at the snow to see the type of grasses underneath, looking for tracks and checking tree trunks for antler rubbings and claw marks that might identify threats or competitors for resources.

Gina appeared at Mei's elbow again. "I'm leaving."

"Have you recorded any data at all?"

She held up her scrawled notes. "Enough. I'm outta here."

"Very well. Go straight to the bus and nowhere else. It should take you less than ten minutes. Straight path, no turns, and Mrs. Chermak will meet you halfway. Is anyone else going?"

"No."

"Then I'll walk with you until we see the bus driver," Mei said.

"You don't need to treat me like I'm a baby," Gina protested. "I come up here all the time."

"Let's just say I don't want to lose anyone up here. Okay?" Mei dialed Mrs. Chermak's cell phone and gave her the message, then signaled to Jack and headed down the trail toward the bus. When she could see a hint of its orange paint through the winter-barren brush and saw Mrs. Chermak waving to them, she stopped and sent the girl on. "There's the bus, Gina. Be sure to stay right there with the driver."

She wasn't very far up the trail again when she thought she heard a faint snicker.

"Time's up," Jack called out. He checked off the list of names on his clipboard against the students huddling at the mouth of the trail, while Mei did the same. "Everyone is accounted for."

Mei looked up from her own clipboard and their eyes locked for an instant. Then she flashed a quick smile and started shepherding the students toward the bus while Jack took up the rear.

Jon, one of the boys who had completed an Eagle Scout project last year, fell in step with Jack. "This was way cool, being out here. I saw eight different kinds of birds, some bear tracks and a set of mountain lion tracks. I wish I'd seen moose, though. They are awesome."

"So you saw bear *and* mountain lion tracks?"

"I completed a tracking badge last fall. I'm sure of it."

"Good job then. There's plenty of wildlife out here, though I'm sure it all headed for the high country when twenty-five noisy teenagers got off the bus."

"What do you think the bear population is in—"

"Jack!" Mei came running up the trail, her hair flying. "I got everyone corralled on the bus, but we have big problems."

"Is someone hurt?"

"I sure hope not." She pulled to a stop and took a ragged breath. "Mrs. Chermak is behind the wheel of the bus in an awfully deep sleep, and I can't rouse her at all. And Gina Meier is missing."

Zach and his deputies arrived within forty-five minutes, followed by an emergency vehicle and two EMTs.

Twenty-five faces were plastered against the windows of the bus while the EMTs moved the silver-haired woman to a gurney, started an oxygen line and took her vitals.

"She acts like she was drugged," Mei said anxiously, hovering over them as they worked. "Nothing I did would wake her. I can't imagine she's the type to take anything illicit, though. Could she have had a stroke?"

"We're taking her in, pronto. If it was drugs, she needs intervention meds ASAP." The other EMT talked on the phone as they rechecked her vitals, then the two of them deftly slid the gurney into the back of the emergency vehicle.

Jack moved closer. "How is she?"

"We ran an EKG and have sent it in. The doctors have already ordered toxicology screenings and more tests at the hospital. She's starting to wake up, but she's really groggy, and she's not oriented to time or place. Zach tried to question her, but she doesn't remember a thing. We're taking her to a hospital on the northeast side of Denver ASAP."

Zach reappeared and quietly conferred with the EMTs again before they took off, sirens wailing. Then he turned to Jack and Mei.

"So what do you think happened?" Jack said.

"Just off the record, the EMTs think she acted as if someone had slipped her some rohypnol. It would account for her sedation and amnesia, if she didn't have a stroke or seizure event of some kind. They've taken her coffee thermos back to the hospital to test it."

"Have you found any trace of Gina?"

"Nothing. The deputies and I have fanned out to check this area, and there's no sign of foul play in the immediate vicinity—no sign of her at all." Zach turned to Mei. "You saw her get on the bus?"

"No. But I escorted her far enough so that we could see Mrs. Chermak and the bus, and then I sent Gina on. There wasn't even a second when Gina wasn't in sight of at least one of us."

Jack cleared his throat. "Her parents?"

"We've called her mother, and she says Gina is never without her cell phone, but she hasn't heard from her. When we dial that number, Gina doesn't answer."

"We have got to let the high school principal know and get these other kids back to school," Mei murmured, her teeth chattering. "And we can't just stand here—we need to look for Gina."

"I already called the principal, and needless to say she sounds pretty upset. Another bus driver is being sent out to take the other kids back and should be here in twenty minutes." Zach turned to Jack. "And I've alerted the search-and-rescue team and requested a dog. Do you have anything with her scent on it here?"

"No. I don't think anything's been left behind."

"Okay, we'll have to ask her mother to bring down some of Gina's clothing to give our dog her scent."

"This seems so strange." Mei frowned. "She was sitting in the first row of seats when we came up here, and I know she had her notebook on the trail. What if the note-book's in there, proving that she actually did get back here? Would someone kidnap her? Was somebody out here all this time, just waiting for a chance to grab one of the kids?"

She ran to the bus and disappeared inside. A hubbub of students' voices arose, and above them, Mei's asking them to settle down.

A moment later, she came back out, her face a grim mask of worry. "Here it is, the notebook she had—the scribbled notes she showed me. But why on earth did she get off that bus—and was it against her will?"

While Mei stayed with the other kids to keep them calm, Zach questioned each of them individually about seeing strangers or anything unusual during the field trip.

Jack went back to searching the area, then started de-tailing the situation to the search-and-rescue team mem-bers and community volunteers as they began showing up.

In the next twenty minutes, nine more volunteers had arrived, along with Gina's mother and a T-shirt she'd grabbed out of Gina's laundry basket.

With bleached blond hair showing dark at the roots and the husky voice of a smoker, she shouldered past Zach and headed for Mei, her face red with anger.

"I'm Barbara Meier. How could you lose my daughter?" she demanded. "How could you bring her up into the wilds like this and then not take care of her? This is *unbeliev-able.*"

Zach came to stand next to Mei. "She was in view of an adult at all times, Mrs. Meier. She refused to stay with the group, but once she was back at the bus with the driver, we don't know what happened. Her notebook was in the bus, yet when the group came back to the bus Gina was gone and the driver was unconscious."

"I suppose he was some predator," Barbara snarled. "Gina probably had to defend herself and run for her life with no one else around."

Zach gave Mei's shoulders a quick, comforting squeeze. "I've already talked to the principal about the driver's background, ma'am. Mrs. Chermak is a sixty-two-year-old grandmother of eight, and she's been a driver in the school district for over twenty years. And there were two other adults with the kids—Jack McCord, the county wild-life biologist, and Ms. Clayton, their teacher."

"Well, they are obviously incompetent, careless people because my daughter is missing. She's in high school, not some toddler who would foolishly walk away. I want her found."

"We're doing everything we can," Zach promised.

The woman turned and thrust a forefinger toward Mei's face, her face mottled and voice rising with every word. "Someone like you shouldn't even have a teaching license if you can't do your job. Don't think this is going to end here, whether they find my daughter or—" She broke off into violent sobs.

One of the women on the search-and-rescue team nodded to Jack, then approached Barbara and gently took her hand to lead her a few yards away.

Zach joined them after a moment. "I'm sorry, but I need to ask you some questions, Mrs. Meier. It's important. If you want to have a better chance of finding your daughter. My patrol car will be a warm place, if you'll come with me."

"O-of course."

Shivers reverberated through Mei's body as she watched

them go. "This is just horrible. That poor mother. And Gina—how could this happen, Jack?"

"The whole thing is strange. Zach says that not one student saw anything suspicious. There's no sign of struggle. Each of the other kids brought backpacks, so they could bring back small samples of dried grasses and brush for their displays. But Gina only brought her purse and she insisted on leaving soon after we got here."

Mei closed her eyes. "After I left her, I thought I heard her snicker. I thought she was just laughing because she'd managed to get out of the field trip. What if she planned to run away?"

"I'm wondering, and Zach is, too. But it could be abduction. Random…or some creep on the internet could've romanced her and convinced her to meet him someplace away from town so he wouldn't be seen when he took her for a 'romantic rendezvous.' No matter what happened, we've got to find her and bring her home."

"I'm so frightened for her." Mei's knees felt wobbly and she wanted to fall into his arms, to rest her head against his chest and feel the beat of his heart, just to draw on his strength. But this was hardly the time or the place. "I'm so glad your team has a search-and-rescue dog."

"She's a great dog and her owner is an excellent handler, but I just hope she can pick up the scent. There was a big scout outing here over the weekend—a good seventy boys and their dads. There are tire tracks everywhere in this parking lot, and people were tramping all over the trails." He looked up at the sky and frowned. "We only have another hour and a half of good daylight, and three or four inches of snow are on the way. I think all of us had better start praying."

Chapter Fourteen

By nine in the evening, Gina's mother had become nearly hysterical, screaming curses and promising that Mei Clayton and Jack McCord were going to face criminal charges if it took every last cent of her savings to make that happen. She finally allowed relatives to take her home and sit with her to wait for news.

By midnight, fifteen members of search-and-rescue teams from the neighboring counties had arrived to help blanket the park, all carrying high-powered flashlights.

They'd found no sign of the missing girl. The dog had followed Gina's scent up the trail to where the students had all been collecting their data and then followed her trail back to the bus, but from there it hit on no other scent trail in any direction.

Bone cold and numb with horror over her thoughts about Gina's possible fate, Mei huddled in the front seat of Zach's patrol car. Even the warmth of its heater couldn't reach the icy fingers that had closed around her heart.

At the sound of footsteps, she looked up and found Zach and Jack approaching the vehicle and behind them followed a number of flashlights bobbing and swaying.

The search was over. And Gina wasn't with them.

Dread twisted her stomach into a tight knot at the grim expressions on the faces as each came into view.

Zach wearily slid into the driver's seat and rested his wrists on the top of the steering wheel. Jack climbed in the driver's side of the backseat. Neither of them spoke, and her fear ratcheted up a notch.

"D-did you find her?" Time seemed to stop as she waited for an answer. "*Tell* me."

His face lined with exhaustion, Zach turned to Mei. "She's been found at a girlfriend's house. They were planning to leave town during the night for Colorado Springs."

"*What?*" Mei stared at him, stunned. "Why would she run away from a school field trip and not just meet her friend later?"

"Oh, they had a good reason."

The low, vehement tone in Zach's voice scared her. "Wh-why?"

"Try a thousand-dollar Visa gift card for each of the girls just to get lost for a little while. Gina was supposed to disappear for a week or so, then come back and claim that she'd been abducted—saying that you and I hadn't answered her calls for help."

Mei stared at him. "That's…that's unbelievable."

Zach nodded. "There was no other scent trail to follow because a car came after her and probably parked next to the bus. Because Gina had already slipped a roofie into that poor bus driver's coffee mug, no one saw it happen. Gina is in custody down at the sheriff's office now, and she's with her mother. Apparently they have magically come up with a lawyer who is there, too."

"Mrs. Meier didn't strike me as the sort of woman who would have one."

"I'm sure this guy was already on call, just in case something went wrong," Jack interjected. "And I'm even more sure that Mrs. Meier isn't paying him. She doesn't look like she would have that kind of money."

"I don't get it." Mei shook her head.

"And I can't believe I didn't see it sooner. It was a scheme to get you out of the picture, Mei. If they got you fired, ruined your reputation, filed high-dollar lawsuits against you and even helped you lose your teaching license, you might just turn tail and leave town." Zach hit the steering wheel with the heel of his hand. "Great-uncle Samuel would love to get his hands on Grandpa George's estate. Three thousand acres of Colorado land and a million and a half dollars must be *almost* as tempting as the joy he'd feel at seeing us all fail. If he runs off just one of us cousins, he has it made. Big victory for his side."

"B-but he's an old man. He came clear out here?"

"Gina said Vincent did," Jack said quietly. "Though I'm sure they planned all of this together."

"Unfortunately, Gina broke down immediately and spilled everything before her lawyer arrived. I'm not sure we could ever use a word of it in court because she was a minor with no representation. Her mother hadn't even arrived yet. And there's probably no concrete evidence." Zach sighed. "I'm not sure we can prove anything. But knowing Vincent, even the way Gina precipitously blurted out her confession was probably part of the big plan."

Jack pulled off his gloves and dropped them on the seat. "When I look back to when my mom married Charley and the time when I once looked up to Vincent, it makes me sick. I never realized what kind of guy he was."

"You were just a boy then." Mei wearily leaned her head against the seat.

"But even as an adult I failed to see him for what he was. I knew he was crafty and self-serving, but I never dreamed he'd sink to this. When I think about how many times I loyally defended him to other people, I want to kick myself into the next county." His voice dripped with anger. "I'll bet he was behind those anonymous notes to you, too. No wonder some people around here have painted me with the same brush."

"It all makes me wish I'd never moved back here."

Zach reached across the seat and squeezed her hand. "But again, that would let Samuel win. If nothing else, we all have to stick together for Arabella so she doesn't lose Grandpa George's house. She deserves it after caring for him all those years. I wouldn't have been able to do it, believe me. He was the most cantankerous, scheming guy on the planet."

"I won't leave. I know the others need their inheritance, and I wouldn't jeopardize what they should receive." She mustered up a sad smile. "It's ironic, really…as a kid I wanted to imagine that I was part of a happy sitcom family, like on TV. Like what I imagined the rest of our family was like. But it was never even close, was it?"

"Not at all, I'm afraid. Though I think our parents tried to shield us from most of what was going on."

"As adults, all of that should be behind us—yet things just keep getting worse," Mei lamented. "When will it ever end?"

"I heard the reports on the television last night about the Meier girl. So they found her safe and sound?"

"Yes." Mei poured her mother another cup of coffee, and topped off her own cup, her nerves still feeling raw and exposed from the night before.

After getting home, it had taken hours to finally fall asleep, then Moose had wanted to go outside at six and her mother had knocked on the door by seven.

"I came over and let your dog out twice yesterday evening."

Surprised and grateful, Mei smiled. "Thanks so much."

"I didn't want him to make messes everywhere, after all." Lisette sipped her coffee. "You must have felt awful after losing a student out there. How on earth did you let it happen?"

Mei had been feeling tired and a little dazed, but now Lisette's words hit her like a jolt of electricity. "You automatically assumed that I lost her. That it was my fault."

Lisette fluttered her fingertips. "Not physically, of course, but you were surely responsible. That mother of hers was on the news, promising to file lawsuits and see you run out of town."

With a sigh, Mei sank back in her chair. The rest of the story hadn't hit the news apparently. Maybe it never would—and Mom had already assumed the worst. But when had that been any different?

"Mom, did you ever really love me?" Maybe it was the emotional exhaustion—the fear, anxiety and shock, followed by a sleepless night. But the words started tumbling from her before she could call them back. "Or was I just an obligation?"

The color drained from Lisette's face. "What?"

"I know you'd wanted children a long time before adopting me. But then Lucas came along two years later—your perfect, white, biological baby. Did you ever wish you could send me back?"

Never—even at her father's funeral—had she seen her mother cry. But now tears shimmered in her eyes and her hand trembled as she settled her coffee cup onto its saucer with a clatter.

"How can you say that?"

"Because I think it's true. I know you tried to do all

the right things. To me, you're my forever mom, and I'll always love you. But…I'm sorry I wasn't what you really wanted."

"What?"

"Did you know that Gina planned to run away? She engineered her escape with help from someone else. But I just heard it in your voice again. You automatically assumed the girl's disappearance was my fault. I guess that, in your eyes, I've been nothing but a series of disappointments."

And it had been the same with Lucas, Mei suddenly realized. Mom had never been satisfied. Neither of them had ever measured up to her standards, and they never would. Until now Mei hadn't recognized the heavy weight of that truth on her shoulders, but now she felt free…light with the knowledge that it hadn't been her own failing, after all.

Rising unsteadily, Lisette came around the table and drew Mei to her feet, then wrapped her arms around her and held her tight for a long moment. "H-have you always thought that?"

Mei melted into her embrace, savoring the rare moment of closeness, and felt bereft when her mother took a step back and held her hands.

Lisette searched her face, her lower lip trembling. "Tell me."

"I'm sorry. I didn't mean it. I'm just…just tired."

"Please."

Mei closed her eyes, wishing she could take every word back. "I…I know I didn't fit in this community—and not in the family, either. Grandpa George made that clear enough, and I never really met the expectations you and Dad had for me, either. But it's okay…I understand."

"No, you don't," Lisette said with a sad smile. "I didn't realize you'd overheard your grandfather, but your dad nearly came to blows with him over his careless remarks. There was no changing George Sr. He was as politically correct as a bulldozer and just as hard to stop." She sighed heavily. "Truth is, he wasn't any more loving toward anyone else in the family. He expressed caring by doing things for people, but he never openly told them about it, and I doubt an 'I love you' or a sincere compliment ever crossed that man's lips."

Somewhere deep in Mei's heart she felt a cold, empty place start to thaw.

"Don't ever think you weren't wanted, Mei. No one wanted a baby more than we did. We tried so long, with one miscarriage after another. Then I had an ectopic pregnancy while we were abroad working as missionaries. The surgery to save my life was done under unimaginable circumstances and we thought precluded the possibility of ever trying again."

"I'm so sorry," Mei whispered.

"Don't be. It was terrible at the time. But when I first held you in my arms, I knew it was God's destiny, and the flood of love that rushed through me just swept me away. *You* were meant to be ours, and we couldn't have loved you more. And yes—when Lucas came along, we loved him just as much because a mother's heart expands to hold every one of her children. Someday you'll see."

Mei's eyes burned with hot tears. She blinked them away.

"As for the rest…" Her mother turned away and went to look out the window, her head bowed. "I've always wanted the best for you, and I've tried to steer you away from harm. But I know I've never been a warm, loving person. The kind of mom a little girl would want. Someday… maybe I'll be able to tell you why—though I'm afraid it might do you more harm than good."

Chapter Fifteen

Jack drove down Hawk Street on Saturday morning, scanning the cars and trucks parked along both sides of the street near the Cowboy Café. *Bingo.*

A gleaming black four-by-four pickup stood above the rest of the vehicles on its high, wide tires, a typical macho image that Vincent had clung to long after the days of his teenage bravado. With him it was all flash and little substance.

Jack parked and strode into the café, heading straight to the back booth Vincent had always favored.

"Even better—three of you are here," Jack growled. "All we need is Samuel to make this group complete."

Pauley and Charley sat on one side of the scarred wooded table, while Vincent sprawled across the bench on the other side, his insolent sneer firmly in place. "We're having a little meeting. Sorry you can't join us," he bit out.

"Believe me, that doesn't break my heart."

Pauley glanced uneasily between Vincent and Jack. "We don't want any trouble here."

"That's right, cowboys." A new middle-aged waitress appeared at Jack's elbow and slammed a hand on her hip as she surveyed the men in the booth. "Any more of it from you three and the owner says you won't be welcome here anymore. Period. Now, is anyone planning to order? If not, you can take this conversation outside."

"Coffees all around for us three," Charley said. "Separate tickets. And I want one of those dandy cinnamon rolls. The ones that are as big as a plate."

Jack moved aside as she started writing on her order pad. "I'll sit over at the counter in a minute or two."

As soon as she left, Jack leveled a look at each of the three men, then zeroed in on Vincent. "I want you to know that the situation with Gina Meier is no secret."

Vincent flicked a bored glance at Jack, then slumped farther down in the booth. "I have no idea what you mean."

"Then let me spell it out for you. You collaborated with her. Enticed her with a slew of cash, so she would run off on her little adventure. I believe it was to damage Mei's reputation in an effort to see her fired."

"Now, why would any of us care?" Vincent drawled. "Though if a teacher is incompetent, it's only in the public interest to see her canned before she can cause any serious harm."

"You have no proof," Charley added with a smug smile. "Going around defaming other people is a good way to land yourself in court."

"There's proof, all right—Gina's own words. Though at least one of you coached her well enough that none of it could be used in court."

Vincent waved a hand dismissively. "Tough luck."

"I want you to leave Mei alone. No more trouble from any of you, understand? Anything happens—*anything*—and I'll know exactly where to look."

"Woo-hoo. I am shaking in my boots, Jack." Vincent snorted. "When did you turn into such a traitor?"

"I'm no traitor. It's just that I'm ashamed of all of you for what you tried to do."

Vincent pulled himself up higher in the booth. "I get it now. You think we're underhanded, trying to get back the part of George Sr.'s money that we deserved in the first place. But you're no better."

"You can bet I'm not trying to hurt people around here."

"No?" Vincent snickered. "We've seen you lately, chasing after plain little Mei Clayton."

"We're friends. Neighbors."

"Yeah, right. You think you'll get your hands on her share if you court her real nice. But tell me, while you're being all self-righteous here—are you any better than us if you go and break that girl's heart?"

Mei entertained Macy on Saturday afternoon, then again on Sunday after church. Each time, Mei stopped inside the little blue farmhouse to visit with Darlene for a few minutes. The woman's ongoing decline was more visible with each passing day.

On Monday, Mei stopped in after school to see the two of them, even though Arabella and Jasmine were scheduled.

"She's asleep," Jasmine said when she opened the door. "But do come in. The hospice nurse is due to stop by in a half hour, so she'll be awake then."

"How is everything?"

"Not so good." Jasmine's eyes glittered with sudden tears as she looked over her shoulder, then lowered her voice. "Darlene is sleeping more and is alert less often. But the doctor upped her pain meds, so that might be part of it. I just wish she could last until after Christmas so poor Macy won't always have to think of her mother's death happening so close to the holidays."

Jasmine led the way from the foyer into the kitchen. "Look who's here, Macy!"

The child looked up from her homework and offered a smile that didn't reach her sad eyes. "Hi, Mei."

"Looks like you have lots and lots of homework, sweetie."

"Spelling and math," she said glumly. "I like reading better."

"Me, too. I'll bet Jasmine is a lot of help, though."

Arabella came around the corner from the living room, her face drawn, but she brightened when her gaze landed on Mei. "I didn't expect to see you here today."

"I just thought I'd stop in and say hello, but I hear Darlene is asleep."

Arabella glanced pointedly at Macy, who was laboriously writing out her spelling words. "She's having a really nice nap right now, so she'll have some more energy later."

Her heart heavy, Mei caught the subtext of Arabella's words. "She's so lucky to have everyone from the Church Care Committee to help."

"Coffee?" Arabella poured a cup from the coffeemaker on the crowded Formica countertop by the sink and handed it over, then poured herself a mugful. "As for the committee, we had a hole in the schedule tomorrow and asked your mom, but she wasn't too keen on the idea."

"As in a flat, no-uncertain-terms 'no'?"

Arabella smiled. "Pretty much. But Kylie and Brooke said they could come, so we're all set."

"For a woman who married a family doctor, my mom always had an aversion to nursing care. Whenever Lucas and I had a case of the stomach wobbles as kids, it was either Dad…or we were on our own."

Arabella finished a sip of coffee, then sputtered. "Stomach wobbles?"

"The only euphemism Mom would use for nausea and its unfortunate results. Everything else was just too graphic for her."

"Oh, my."

"How are the Thanksgiving plans coming along?"

Jasmine looked up from Macy's spelling list, opened a pink notebook on the table and grinned. "Super. Just eight more days to go. I've sent the invitations to everyone on the other side of the family tree and have the rest ready to send out tomorrow. I have the town meeting hall reserved because nobody's house is big enough."

"And none of us want a brawl in our dining room," Arabella said drily.

"That isn't going to happen," Jasmine shot back with a grin. "We're checking shotguns and rifles at the door."

She ran her finger down a list in her notebook. "My centerpieces are made. I borrowed the tablecloths already, and they are washed and ironed. There are enough tables and folding chairs at the hall, so I didn't have to rent them. The food is all set, too. Between what I prepare and what people bring, we should be able to feed dozens of people with ease."

"You are an amazing woman, Jasmine." Mei grinned. "You're really going to feed that many people?"

"Counting all the kids, yes. Maybe more. I just hope they all come, or I'll be stuck with four twenty-three-pound turkeys and we'll be eating it for the next year."

"And you're planning a wedding? Your life makes me dizzy, by the way."

"That's pretty much in place, too." Jasmine's smile turned soft and dreamy. "Christmas Eve will be the best day of my life, bar none. Cade and I are so going to prove everyone wrong when we celebrate our fiftieth wedding anniversary and are still going strong."

"Good for you. I hope I'm around to see it."

"We heard the news about that high school girl, by the way." Arabella lowered her voice. "Zach came by the house Sunday night and told us everything because he said it wasn't fair that the radio and TV newscasters cast all the blame on you and Jack."

"Only the fact that she was missing for a while was given to the news people."

"Personally, I think the public should hear about what that girl did, even if she is a minor. It's just wrong that the gossips are all saying that she was lost because you and Jack were careless."

"Given that her mother's a relation of Vincent's, I'd guess the two of them talked Gina into the whole scheme and then added a hefty bribe so she couldn't say no. But she's too young to have that whole unfortunate mess follow her forever." Mei glanced at her cousin. "And you know as well as I do that no one ever forgets a juicy bit of gossip in a small town."

"So where are the charges against Vincent and Gina's mother?"

"If there's ever enough evidence, then maybe there will be," she said with a shrug. "But I'm not holding out hope."

"When I hear talk about either of you, I step right in… believe me. Too many people have been wrong about Cade and Jack all these years, and it's time someone on our side of the family stood up for what's right. You want to know one good thing about Gina's disappearance?" Arabella asked.

"I can't think of a single thing," Mei admitted drily.

"Well, this time Vincent's schemes ended up being directed at Jack and one of us, and maybe now people can see that those two *aren't* on the same team…and never were."

* * *

Arabella had said there was one good thing that had come out of Gina's disappearance, but she was wrong. There were two, and Mei was staring at all six-foot-two of the second one across a dinner table right now and silently counting her blessings.

"I can't believe we're doing this," she murmured, leaning over the table.

"Having a real, honest-to-goodness dinner out?"

"Right. I mean—I'm happy you invited me, Jack. After all we've had to deal with, I never imagined we'd be sitting here with candlelight and crystal, instead of facing a room full of teenagers or some crisis."

"I figured that we deserved this." He cut the final piece of his tenderloin in half. "And honestly, I've wanted to do this for a long time."

"I know you're kidding, but it's sweet of you to say that."

He caught her gaze. "Ten years, in fact."

"Now I do know you're kidding."

"Do you remember homecoming, senior year?" he asked.

"Vaguely. I think our parents took Lucas and me with them for four days in Aruba over that weekend."

"I'd just about gathered the courage to ask you out, but I heard you would be gone anyway. And then...well..." His mouth lifted in a wry grin. "Things changed."

She laughed. "I'll bet. If I remember correctly, you always had a flock of girls circling around you. If any of them caught wind of that near defection, she probably swooped in like a hawk and didn't let you go."

"Funny...I don't remember that at all."

She knew he was still teasing, but it still felt incredible to be out with him. As an awkward teenager, she wouldn't have ever believed she'd be here, enjoying a wonderful meal and the chance to banter with the man she'd had a crush on throughout high school.

But this wasn't just a crush anymore.

"I saw Jasmine and Arabella at Darlene Perry's house yesterday. I remember thinking she and Cade were awfully young to get married, but that girl certainly has made plans for the future."

"When Cade told me about their engagement, I spent the next two months trying to talk him out of it. I nearly ruined our relationship because of my strong opinions."

"You were only trying to help him make the right choice. I'm sure he knew that, even if he did rebel against what you were trying to say."

Jack toyed with his fork for a long moment, his expression pensive, then he looked at Mei over the flickering candle between them. "Now I honestly envy him for finding the love of his life and for having the strength to follow his dreams no matter what anyone said to stop him. Some of us don't have that much gumption. Just think of the years that are wasted that way. Missed opportunities for true happiness. And you can't get any of it back."

So apparently Jack had had his own share of disappointments over the years. Which one of the young beauties orbiting around him had broken his heart?

"Maybe the right person hasn't really come along yet."

He eyed her thoughtfully. "Oh, she did."

"And there was no one else afterward?"

"Now and then. Nothing serious. So how about you?" The teasing glint was back in his eyes. "How did you make it to the grand old age of twenty-eight without some dude taking you off the market?"

She pushed a piece of her chicken parmesan back and forth on her plate for a while, sorting out her thoughts.

"I guess I never really felt emotionally attached enough. They were all nice guys, good friends…but whenever I had to move somewhere else the relationships didn't survive, and none of them broke my heart when they ended." *Because none of them were ever like you.* "I think my destiny is to become a much-feared spinster teacher with a hairnet and wielding a ruler."

He laughed. "That I can see because you must weigh all of a hundred pounds."

A waiter noiselessly appeared at Mei's elbow. "Would you two care for dessert? Coffee?"

Jack raised a brow, but Mei shook her head. "This has been lovely, but I have school tomorrow and you have an early appointment—and we both have the parent open house at school, too. Plus, Moose is probably dying to get outside. I'd better get home."

Light snow was drifting like falling diamonds beneath the streetlamps as Jack drove slowly down Railroad Street, then turned up Grosbeak toward Silver Creek.

He surprised her—and turned her insides to Jell-O—when he got out and walked her to her door. She fumbled with her keys, suddenly feeling as shy and uncertain as a sixteen-year-old on a first date.

A loud woof echoed from inside the cottage when she slid the key in the lock.

"I'll bet that dog registers on the Richter scale when he barks," Jack said, standing aside when she let Moose bound out of the house. "Does the sound ever break your stemware?"

She laughed. "Almost."

They stood together watching the dog joyously bound through the snowdrifts in the yard, his tongue lolling and tail wagging.

Jack caught her mittened hand in his. "He has got to be

the happiest dog I've ever seen. Of course, he chose his new house and owner, and she did agree. Some guys are just lucky that way."

"And all it took was sprawling across my porch so I would trip on him on my way to work."

"If that's the way to your heart, it doesn't sound too bad…as long as a guy has health insurance, anyway," he said with a wink.

Did she dare read anything more into his words? She looked up at him and felt a flutter in the vicinity of her heart. If they'd both stayed in town, would he have ever asked her out? Was there a chance that they might have ended up together all this time?

"I really enjoyed the evening," she murmured. "Thanks for dinner."

Jack smiled down at her. "Maybe we can do this again sometime."

"I'd like that."

He started down the porch steps. Stopped. Then he spun on his heel and came back to drop a kiss on her mouth, leaving her feeling dazed and giddy and more than a little tingly from head to toe.

And then he was gone.

Chapter Sixteen

By the end of the school day on Friday, Mei felt herself buzzing with anticipation over the schoolwide parent-teacher open house starting at seven o'clock.

Despite the tumultuous end to the field trip on Wednesday, the students had rallied afterward, working on their data and displays both at home and in class, and they'd all done a wonderful job.

Even Gina had come up with a minimal effort on the endangered least tern, though she'd been subdued since returning to school the day after the field trip and had kept her eyes downcast throughout class.

Since the last bell at the end of the day, Mei had been cleaning and rearranging the classroom to best display the projects from the class. Time flew by, and before she knew it, most of her students had filtered back into class, setting up their displays and rehearsing their one-minute presentations for the parents who would start arriving in fifteen minutes.

Mei floated along the perimeter of the room, armed with a stapler and cellophane tape as she praised each student as they worked on their setup.

Sensing the girl's deep embarrassment, Mei mustered

up a bright smile when she reached Gina's haphazard poster board with an internet article stapled in the lower corner and a photocopied picture of a least tern fastened in the center.

"Did you enjoy reading up on this bird, Gina?"

The girl was just about as tall as Mei, but she was overweight and awkward, and her frizzy blond hair added several inches to her height. With her ratty tennis shoes and faded sweatshirt, the complete package was that of a person who had few resources at home.

She picked at her chipped nail polish. "It was all right."

"I'm really happy that you're here tonight. I know a lot of the students live a long ways out in the country, so it's quite a trip back into town for something like this."

"I stayed."

"You stayed in town? That was a good idea."

She picked at her nail polish with even greater intensity, and Mei thought she saw a teardrop fall on the girl's sleeve.

"Did you stay here, at school?"

Gina nodded.

"Did you have supper?"

She didn't respond.

"You know, I brought a sack lunch for tonight, but I didn't finish it all. I still have a yogurt and an apple, and if you'd take them off my hands I wouldn't have to bother taking them home."

Gina flashed a quick, almost hostile sideways look at Mei. "Why would you be nice to me?" she mumbled.

"Why not? You're one of my students, and I'd guess you'd prove to be one of the brighter ones, if you applied yourself. It would be fun to see you bloom. If not in my class, then in one you really like."

Mei started on to the next display, then had an uneasy

feeling and turned back to Gina. "If by chance your parents are really busy and can't come tonight, let me know. I'm sure we can arrange a ride home for you."

At the next table, Jon was carefully gluing prairie grass in a graceful arc over the top edge of his plains sharp-tailed grouse display. Mei suppressed the impulse to whistle in appreciation. If this boy didn't end up in advertising or some aspect of the art world, he would be hiding his light under a bushel.

"Very nice, Jon," a deep, familiar voice came from behind Mei.

She turned and came face-to-face with Jack. "I'm so glad you came! The students all loved having you involved in our class."

He smiled. "I enjoyed it more than I thought I would."

"Have you looked at all the displays?"

"Just got here." He followed her around the room, talking to each student, asking questions at each stop as he admired their work.

By the time they got to Gina's spot, she was nowhere to be seen.

"She's really uncomfortable with me," Mei whispered. "So she may feel even more shy with you. If she comes back, let's just give her some space."

The parents started flooding in, reviewing the projects from their own children's classes and then moving through the endangered species displays. She'd seen many of the parents at church or the grocery. She spied a taller man and tried to place him, then realized he was one of Zach's deputies.

"I'll just get out of the way," Jack said as he moved to a corner of the room and leaned a shoulder against the blackboard.

Most of the parents introduced themselves and peppered Mei with questions about the classes and how their children were doing—even though it wasn't an evening set up for individual reviews.

She didn't see trouble coming until she finished answering a parent's question and turned to find Barbara Meier forging through the crowd, followed by a husky, bald man sporting tattoos covering the side of his neck.

"I know," she said loudly. "It's just a miracle that my daughter is with me after that field trip. No one was watching out for her—no one cared. My poor baby was lost for *hours*."

The other parents shifted uncomfortably, most trying to avoid looking her way as she continued to make a scene. Some quietly slipped out the door with an apologetic nod in Mei's direction. Some frowned, obviously believing every word.

Mei looked over at Jack and shook her head firmly, then closed her eyes briefly for a quick, silent prayer, hoping he would stay put and not make things worse by coming to her rescue.

But Barbara slid a smug look in Mei's direction and then raised her voice even more. "I don't understand *why* they don't hire competent, experienced teachers who care about their jobs. I mean, how hard is it to keep track of a few teenagers and—"

A soft wail came from the open doorway. Every other noise in the room stopped as everyone turned toward the door.

It was Gina, her face reddened with embarrassment, her mouth open in horror. She looked over at Mei as tears started to fall down her cheeks. "It isn't true," she whispered. "None of it's true. I-I'm so sorry, Ms. Clayton."

Her mother shoved her way through the other parents.

"Gina, you're overwrought. Let's go to the bathroom and cool down. A little splash of water on your face and—"

"No." Gina shook her head slowly, her jaw trembling. "You *made* me leave the field trip so you could get Ms. Clayton in trouble." Her voice rose. "And it was all about money. I-I've never been so embarrassed in my whole *life!*"

Mei eased to the side of the room, grabbed the intercom mike and spoke quietly into it, thankful that the office staff was here for this event.

Most of the parents had now filtered out of the room, taking the students and their displays with them. The deputy, dressed in street clothes, stood at the door with his cell phone at his ear, eyeing Barbara with considerable interest.

A second later Mrs. Baker, the principal, arrived and gently rested her hands on Gina's shoulders. "How are you, dear?" she murmured. "Is everything all right in here?"

Gina turned into her embrace, crying.

Barbara spun toward Mei, her eyes flashing with contempt. "It's all your fault. I never should have let my daughter sign up for this class. Because of you—"

"Enough." The deputy gave Barbara's companion a searing look that made him stumble back a step, then he turned back to her. "I have a patrol car coming for you so we can go down to the sheriff's office and get to the bottom of this. If I were you, I wouldn't say another word to this teacher, much less stand in public and make unfounded accusations."

Her heart breaking for Gina, who was still sobbing against Mrs. Baker's shoulder, Mei went to the doorway and laid a hand on the teen's arm. "I'm so sorry about this. But I want you to know that the other kids will realize that none of this was your fault. And I know we'll all be glad to have you back in class."

Mei looked over her shoulder at the deputy. "What about Gina? I don't know if she'll be okay going home if her mother is this…um…upset. Or with that guy, either."

"Her boyfriend," Gina whispered brokenly. "But m-my aunt and uncle live in town. I go there a lot. I can go to their house."

"Good—we just want you to be safe."

Long after the deputies took Barbara and Gina away and all of the parents were gone, Mei stood slumped against her desk, talking quietly to the principal.

Jack watched from out in the hallway, affording them privacy, but what he really wanted to do was to walk in there and whisk her out to her SUV because she looked utterly exhausted.

When the two of them finally came out, Mei had pulled on her cranberry jacket and held her purse. She locked the door behind her.

The principal nodded to Jack, then strode away toward the central offices, her heels clicking against the polished terrazzo floor.

"I'd be happy to sweep you off your feet and carry you out to your car," he offered. "You look worn-out."

"I am, but I'm going outside on my own power. I don't even want to think about all the rumors that would fly if you did that."

He fell into step as she walked toward the exit. "Might keep life interesting."

That earned a short laugh. "Believe me—my life has been *way* too interesting lately. I'm starting to crave boredom. Preferably following twelve hours of sleep."

"What did your principal have to say?"

Mei sighed. "It has been a little rocky for her around here. Dozens of agitated phone calls from parents who are worried about security. Questioning why I was hired. Some demands that I ought to be fired immediately."

Jack didn't have to guess where some of those calls had come from. "I'm sorry it went that far."

"Me, too. She understands the situation. I explained in depth about how a lot of people could profit greatly if I left town. But she also has to be concerned about a safe, healthy school environment. Another ruckus like this one would probably make her seriously consider whether the benefits of having me here would outweigh the costs."

"There might be other jobs."

"And other opportunities for someone like Vincent to strike again." She sighed. "I just wish I was independently wealthy and didn't need to have a job here. It would make things a whole lot easier."

Jack walked beside her for a few moments, thinking. "I understand there used to be a part-time secretary at the wildlife biologist's office here. Maybe I can find some funding."

She smiled up at him. "I know where you're going with this, but this isn't your obligation. So far, I still have my position at the high school. If something changes, then I'll just look around until something else turns up. Who knows—maybe I can get a job bussing tables at the Cowboy Café."

They walked out of the building and into the chilly darkness toward the parking lot, where a single security lamp cast a pool of light on the sidewalk.

Jack hesitated, then draped an arm around her shoulders as they walked. Even under her bulky jacket, she felt so delicate, so vulnerable that he wished he would never have to let her go. "You're wrong about the obligation,

Mei. Maybe I'm not related to Vincent and the others, but I was once pretty close to them. If they try to harm someone I care about, I'm going to step in."

She looked at him in alarm. "You won't do anything rash."

"As in 'armed and dangerous'? No. But they're a crafty lot, and they've gotten away with far too much over the years. It's time that someone stood in their way."

Twelve hours of sleep had sounded wonderful yesterday evening. But with a massive dog standing at the side of her bed at seven in the morning, its head resting on her pillow, that wasn't going to happen.

"Woof."

The soft sound ruffled Mei's long hair, tickling her nose.

"Woof."

She opened one eye and found herself looking into Moose's massive jaws as he yawned. "If you're tired and I'm tired, why aren't we both sleeping?"

Knowing he wouldn't give up because he needed to go out, she scuffed into her slippers, shouldered into her heavy robe and trudged blearily out to the kitchen. "Here you go," she called out as she opened the door.

Lisette stood there with Albert in her arms, her hand poised ready to knock.

Mei blinked. "Good morning."

"I'm here because I just couldn't sleep. We need to talk."

There would be no going back to bed, Mei realized. She let Moose back inside, then went to the counter and started a pot of coffee. "Toast? Eggs? Oatmeal?"

Lisette hung her coat by the door and slipped off her snow boots, then picked up Albert and held him close.

"Nothing, really. But thanks. Later on I'll have a Saturday morning brunch with Maude, from church."

"What's wrong?"

"I…I haven't been completely truthful with you all these years. It was for the best. I think any parent would agree. But now I realize—" She took a slow breath. "I realize from our last conversation that unspoken feelings can be taken in the wrong way and lead to pain one never intended. If I don't speak up and try to save you from what I went through, you and I will both come to regret it."

"What are you talking about?"

"I've seen you with Jack McCord a number of times, and I am worrying so much about you making a terrible mistake. It disappoints me that you haven't listened when I've tried to warn you about him."

Mei couldn't believe they were having this conversation *again*. "He's a nice man, Mother," she said defensively.

"You must listen to me. You can't trust him…he's a *liar*. He showed it time and time again, running with Vincent's pack of friends as a teenager, and people don't change. Character doesn't just come out of nowhere when you grow up."

"He doesn't need to change. He wasn't like those other boys."

"Why do you think I'm so concerned?" her mother persisted.

"I—"

A foggy image flitted through Mei's memory.

Awakening late at night to the sound of raised voices. Her mother pleading. Intense, heated words.

She'd forgotten. Pushed the memories far away because they'd threatened everything that made her world seem safe and secure.

"Your father was unfaithful, Mei. Your upstanding,

righteous, pillar-of-the-community father was unfaithful for years and years before I found out, and he never changed once I knew. The lies could trip so easily off his tongue and they would be so believable that I second-guessed myself all the time." Her words were tinged with bitterness. "There was always a reason—a good excuse. And because I was afraid of losing my home and losing you and Lucas, I didn't have the backbone to make it stop."

Mei felt everything she'd known about her father start to crumble. He'd been the parent to reprimand, the one to establish rules and an iron-clad moral code for what it meant to be a Clayton. He was the one who marched the family to church every week and made sure they were in their Sunday best. He'd been intolerant of deceit.

And yet, if Mom was right, his own life had been a lie.

"I wanted to explain because I don't want you to risk following in my footsteps. And I wanted to explain, in part, why I might have seemed…distant…when you were growing up. It was never about you. You have always been loved beyond measure, even if I failed to show it." Her mouth twisted. "It was all about me. Of course, Vern had pills for everything, and clearing up a little problem with depression was easy enough. And I figured that if a few worked, a few more might be better. So many of those early years are just a fog to me now."

Mei had always thought she didn't belong. Thought that she wasn't loved because she was different from everyone else. But it hadn't been that at all.

Instead, her idyllic, beautiful home had been a complete sham, with her handsome, womanizing father, and an ethereally lovely mother who was lost in a haze of medications.

Mei rubbed her eyes, trying to sort through the revelations that had just changed everything she knew about herself and her family.

"There's more." Lisette dropped into the chair next to Mei's, her eyes haunted and apologetic. "I am so sorry, but there is more."

Mei stared at her. "I don't think I want to know."

"I wouldn't be telling you this now if I didn't have to. But there's not much time."

"Are...are you ill?" Mei felt another piece of her world start to shatter and fall away.

Lisette shook her head. "I'd always known of your father's affairs. But no matter how much it hurt, I kept his secrets while he was alive and protected his memory after he was gone—for myself, and for you and Lucas because I wanted to guard our own honor, even if he had none."

She pulled a small, folded piece of yellowed paper from her pocket and pressed it into Mei's palm. "This was in your father's pocket the day he died. Do with this what you will."

"I—I don't understand."

"I believe you have a half sister...but if you want answers, you're going to have to move fast. Because her mother is about to die."

Chapter Seventeen

As Mei drove out to Darlene Perry's house she called her cousins to find out where everyone was.

Brooke and Gabe had taken Macy for an outing, so fortunately the child wouldn't be home when Mei arrived, but both Arabella and Vivienne were already at Darlene's house.

Thankful that two of her cousins were there, Mei pulled into the drive, tapped on the back door and let herself inside. The two woman were carefully rolling Darlene over to lay on a different side in her hospital bed, so Mei waited quietly in the kitchen until they joined her.

Arabella peeled off her disposable vinyl gloves, reached for a cup of coffee sitting on the counter and put it into the microwave. "You said you needed to talk to us about something important."

"I'm not even sure where to begin. What do you know about Macy's father?"

"Believe me, we would all like to know." Vivienne turned to slip off her gloves and wash her hands at the sink. "Darlene has refused to tell anyone, and there's not a father listed on Macy's birth certificate. She'll only say that the man died long ago and that she's done her best to be a good parent. End of story."

"Well, I just spent a few of the most difficult hours of my life talking to my mom. She discussed a lot of personal things, but then started telling me about how my dad had lots of affairs. I was just stunned."

Vivienne and Arabella exchanged glances.

"We've both heard about his affairs…just by overhearing things at family gatherings and such," Arabella said as she retrieved her cup from the microwave. "It wasn't common knowledge in the community, though."

Mei retrieved the folded piece of paper from her purse. "Well, my mom says this paper was in my father's pocket the day he died. She kept it secret all these years because she wanted to protect his memory and, I suspect, salvage her pride. But when she started working on the Church Care Committee and learned of Darlene's condition, she thought it was time to divulge it."

Mei unfolded it on the table. "All it says is 'Darlene, 24 Snow Road,' with 'baby' underlined twice. But the first time I saw Macy, I noticed her features reminded me a lot of Brooke's school pictures when she was about that age. What do you think?"

Arabella nodded. "Jonathan once told me that he thought the same thing."

"And Darlene was thrilled when Brooke said she would take Macy in and adopt her…well, when the time comes," Vivienne added.

Mei tapped the note on the table. "This poor little girl will soon be an orphan. Maybe Lucas could be DNA tested, in lieu of our dad, but I don't understand enough about genetics to know if that would be enough proof. Would it rule out the other men in our family tree?" Mei faltered, thinking about her missing brother. "But if this note means what I think it does, Darlene's confirmation that my dad was Macy's father would give the child a true connection to us by blood—with cousins and aunts and uncles."

Vivienne rested a hand on Mei's arm. "How do you feel about all of this?"

"I don't even know yet. I'm still reeling with shock after discovering that the dad I thought I knew was really a complete stranger. But Macy's welfare is what we need to think about now. Do you think Darlene is up to answering this question?"

Vivienne looked pensively toward the darkened living room. "Every day she fails a little more. Sleeps more. The hospice nurses say it's part of her gradual decline as her organs shut down. She isn't going to get better. I don't know if we dare wait."

"But what about the stress?" Arabella frowned. "Do we dare upset her?"

A long silence fell between them, then Vivienne cleared her throat. "I don't think there's even a question of what to do. We need to ask—for Macy's sake."

An hour later Mei heard a soft, weak moan. "Is she waking up?"

"She does that in her sleep sometimes, but I'll check on her." Arabella's forehead was lined with worry. "Vivienne, I think you've been here the most and have the most rapport. If you want to talk to her, Mei and I can serve as witnesses."

"I'll ask. If she's relieved to have the weight of this finally off her shoulders, maybe she'd agree to being recorded, just so we would have additional proof. There's a voice recorder function on my phone."

Mei nodded. "But the only people who would contest

her words would be my dad's heirs. Mom wanted me to come here. I wouldn't argue, and I can't imagine Lucas would, either. This just narrows down whose DNA should be tested."

The vertical blinds in the living room were drawn against the harsh winter sunshine, though thin bars of light leaked through the vanes and painted the room with bars reminiscent of a jail.

Vivienne approached the bed first and rested a gentle hand on Darlene's frail arm. "Darlene. Can you hear me? Are you awake?"

She shifted her weight and moaned again. Her eyes fluttered open. "Vivienne. Is—is Macy all right?"

"She's fine. She's off on an adventure with Brooke and Gabe. I think they were taking her to Erin Fields's horse rescue to see a donkey, and then they planned to go sledding and have lunch at the café."

Darlene rolled her head a few millimeters, her mouth twisting in a grimace that might have been intended as a smile. "Arabella. And…Mei."

"You have lots of visitors this morning, hon. It's a beautiful, sunny Saturday morning. Thanksgiving is just five days away. Though it seems more like January with all the snow we've been having."

Darlene nodded almost imperceptibly.

"We have a question for you. It's really important and it's about your daughter." Vivienne curled a hand around Darlene's and smiled. "You know that she will always have a home with Brooke and Gabe. A good, loving home. But we've come across some evidence. A note from long ago that makes us think that Vern Clayton was actually her real dad. Is that true?"

Darlene's eyes opened wider. She drew in an agitated breath, then started to cough, flailing her free hand as if she were warding off an enemy. "No. That isn't…isn't true." Her rusty voice rose with each word.

Vivienne waited for Darlene's rapid breathing to calm down. "We don't want to upset you, but leaving your daughter with knowledge of her true father would be a blessing to her, don't you think? Lisette Clayton thought the note might be proof that Dr. Clayton was Macy's dad. No one is blaming you, Darlene. No one will hold the truth against you or your daughter. Whoever the man was, it can only be a good thing if Macy knows."

Darlene rolled her head away from them and faced the wall, her eyes closed. "No."

Vivienne looked over her shoulder at Mei and Arabella and shook her head, then tucked the blankets around Darlene's shoulders. "It's okay, Darlene. You rest now…just rest."

Out in the kitchen the three women gathered around the small kitchen table.

"I don't understand it," Arabella said softly. "Darlene has been so relieved to have Macy placed with a Clayton family. She has said it a dozen times just to me. She is so protective of her daughter that I would think she'd grasp at this chance to create stronger ties between Macy and our family."

Vivienne nodded. "Even if Vern wasn't Macy's dad, this was a perfect chance for her to give Macy a true legacy. Why wouldn't she tell us the name of Macy's father?"

Mei looked thoughtfully at both of them. "Considering how weak she is, her strong reaction conveyed an awful lot of emotion. It reminded me of the line from Hamlet that's always being misquoted. 'The lady doth protest too much, methinks.' But the next big question is *why?*"

All the way back into town, Mei's thoughts spun. Her mother's confession. Her dad's lies. The fact that she'd been in town over three weeks already, yet there'd been not a single word about her brother.

Her nightmares about him were occurring more frequently. Visions of him being lost and hurt, trying to escape the Florida swamps, while alligators followed him relentlessly, closing in one inch at a time with the promise of a terrifying death waiting in their powerful jaws.

She needed answers. She'd prayed for answers. Why hadn't there been any news?

Back in town she drove down Eagle Street past the sheriff's office, but Zach's car wasn't out front. Why wasn't he doing anything? Frustrated, she pulled off the street and scrolled through the phone book in her cell phone, then called his private number. He answered on the third ring.

"Mei. I suppose you want to know about Barbara Meier."

"With everything else that has happened in the past twenty-four hours, I haven't even thought about her."

"Everything all right?" he asked.

"Fair. We can talk later if you're busy doing something right now."

"This is a good time. Just so you know, on Friday night Gina insisted on giving us a statement with her lawyer present, and the D.A. is racking up a number of charges against her mother. We also found some drugs on Barbara and obtained a search warrant on her rental house." He cleared his throat. "We found some meth lab paraphernalia in the basement, so I think Barbara and her tattooed buddy are going to be out of the picture for a long time. Gina said she was just sick of all the lies."

Mei thought about Gina, masking her pain with her sarcasm and false bravado, and her heart wrenched. "What will happen to her?"

"It's all being sorted out, but she's a juvenile and it's pretty clear to me that her lovely mom pushed her into that plot to discredit you. Gina's paternal aunt and uncle are good, solid people, and they want her to stay with them long-term."

"That's good news." Mei gripped the phone a little tighter. "What about Vincent?"

"The D.A. doesn't think we have enough yet to charge him for anything. But maybe this situation will be enough warning that he'll finally get his act together."

"And Lucas—have you heard anything at all?"

"Nope. I've been following up every other day with the police chief down there, but there's been no news at all. I'll call them again on Monday."

Disappointment washed through her. "Thanks, Zach. I know you're doing your best."

She debated about going to the Cowboy Café for breakfast. To Mom's for coffee, to tell her about Darlene. Or just going home and going back to bed.

But after a moment's indecision, she headed for Jack's cabin. Of all the places in town, there was nowhere else she wanted to be right now.

She just hoped that he would be home.

"I suppose you're real pleased with yourself," Pauley spat. He glanced around the log cabin housing the wildlife biologist's office. "Fancy degree. Fancy job."

"I'm not sure where this is going," Jack said mildly, looking up from his computer screen. "But if you stopped in to hand out compliments, thanks."

"You heard about Gina and her mother blabbering about Vincent. This time with their lawyer in the room. Why couldn't those two leave well enough alone?"

"Maybe they realized that telling the truth was important."

Pauley grunted in disagreement. "You know it's gonna hurt Vincent's reputation around here."

"What reputation? This is just more of the same for him."

"But it diminishes our family name all the more. I'm the mayor. I have to be concerned about such things."

Jack kept typing up his report on his latest bear count. "As I see it, you aren't so concerned about doing something bad. You just don't want it widely known."

"That's not true at all," Pauley blustered. "Not true at all."

"You've all got a great opportunity for some positive PR coming right up. Though I don't expect you'll have the courage to show up."

"You mean that ridiculous Thanksgiving dinner."

"That's exactly what I mean." Jack stopped typing and swiveled his chair toward Pauley. "The whole lot of you should attend. Show you can be civil for three hours. Make nice conversation. Be interested in all of those people you count as enemies, and maybe you'll find a lot of common ground. And then this ridiculous feud can finally come to an end."

"Maybe we will—if only to show *you* that you're wrong." He started for the door, then turned back, his mouth twisted in a leer. "So tell me—how's that big romance of yours coming along? Got your hooks into that little gal yet?"

"It's not a big romance. And I'm certainly not trying to get at her money."

Pauley chortled. "Glad to hear it because I have it on good authority that your little Mei Clayton has no intention of staying around here—and she wants absolutely no ties to you or anyone else that might complicate a speedy departure once her twelve-month sentence is up here. So, sonny, don't think that you'll have a chance of holding her back."

Chapter Eighteen

When she drove up Bluebird Lane, crossed the Silver Creek bridge and turned into the lane leading to the cabin housing the Clayton County Forest Service offices, Mei smiled to herself and sighed with relief. Jack's county SUV was still parked out front, along with a car she didn't recognize, but at least he wasn't off in the mountains somewhere.

Over the course of the past month she'd taught classes with him, faced difficult situations and had enjoyed some of the most wonderful evenings, just talking with Jack over cups of coffee and Arabella's pie.

Her mother was dead wrong.

Through it all she'd come to see him as so much more than the handsome boy back in high school. He wasn't anything like Vincent, even if her mother couldn't see it. He was a thoughtful, intelligent and honorable man, with a remarkable level of patience for defiant teenagers—and that alone ought to give him gold stars in anyone's grade book. Not to mention that his wicked sense of humor charmed her completely.

She already knew their relationship didn't have a long-term future, but she was going to pray that it lasted at least until she left town. She would then treasure the memories because she already knew that no one else would ever measure up…and no one else would ever be able to capture her heart.

She waited in her car until Jack's visitor came out and drove away, then turned off her engine and headed inside the building.

She found Jack frowning at his computer, with a tall stack of files at his elbow and a clipboard next to his keyboard. "This is Saturday. No rest for the wicked?"

He looked up at her and smiled, though his smile didn't reach his eyes. "Hello, Mei."

She cocked her head and studied him. "Is something wrong?"

"Not at all. I'm just trying to catch up on things. I've had a lot going on lately."

He didn't automatically invite her to sit down or ask what she was doing for lunch, and now she felt a frisson of unease. "I…um, thought you might like to hear that Gina has provided statements against her mother and Vincent. The deputies also found drug paraphernalia in Barbara Meier's basement, so we won't be faced with her verbal attacks in the future. Gina has decided to move in with an aunt."

Jack shook his head. "I feel sorry for her. It's going to be humiliating for her to come back to school on Monday after her mother's scene during the open house."

"If it were middle school she would probably beg to move to a different district. But kids aren't quite as cruel by the time they're seniors in high school." Mei smiled. "I think she'll be surprised at how much the kids try to befriend her after this."

"I'm glad, then." He looked at his computer monitor, clicked his mouse, then pulled his gaze away from the screen. "So…what's it like being back home? Is everything else going okay?"

"No word on Lucas, and if I don't hear something soon I'm going down to the Everglades myself."

"You're not serious."

"Actually, I am. I don't think anyone else really cares. And on the home front, I had a long and difficult conversation with my mom."

He glanced at her. "How did *that* go?"

"Surprisingly, I think we've finally made a connection after all these years. That was one of my main reasons for coming back here for a while."

"So you found common ground."

"More than we've had. I've always wanted to have a better relationship but just never thought it was possible."

Jack swiveled his chair toward her, and an unnamed emotion crossed his face. "So after you're done here, you'll go back to your job in San Francisco?"

He seemed distracted…distant. He was probably just trying to be polite, even though he had work to do. Maybe he was gently letting her know that he really wasn't as interested in her as she'd hoped.

Uneasiness laced with guilt started to twist her stomach into an uncomfortable knot. "My principal said she would hire me back, yes. It's a wonderful school. My best job ever."

"That's great, Mei."

Just thinking about the last kiss they'd shared still had the power to send tingles clear to her toes, and being with him made her feel happy and alive. She wanted to ask him about what he felt for her and tell him how she felt, but memories of her humiliation in high school slammed into her thoughts and held her back. How pathetic would it be to throw herself at the feet of someone who was only trying to be kind?

She'd see the same gentle sympathy in his eyes that he'd offered back in school, and she would want to die right on the spot.

"I guess I'd better be going." She waited for a split second, hoping he might respond with a suggestion that they meet later, but he only gave her a weary smile. "See you at the Thanksgiving dinner?"

He shrugged. "Not sure I'll make it."

"I hope so, Jack."

But he was already focused on his computer screen and back to work. And in that deafening silence, she walked out of the door.

Mei had said that she would go after Lucas herself. Given the determined look in her eyes when she said it, Jack had no doubt that she would try—and then could get herself caught up in a situation that could potentially be far beyond what she could handle.

Grabbing his cell phone, Jack dialed Zach's personal number. *Bingo.*

"Your cousin Mei is headed for a lot of trouble," Jack said, pacing back and forth in front of the café, his cell phone at his ear.

Zach cleared his throat. "Vincent?"

"No…this time it's Lucas. She says she's going to head for Florida and go after him herself if she doesn't hear something soon, and I have no doubt that she would do exactly that."

"If the cops and two private investigators haven't been able to turn up any clues, what chance would she have? She's a teacher, not a P.I."

"Just try to tell her that," Jack said. "She's convinced

that no one cares enough to really look for him. I saw the determination in her eyes. I agree that she has far less chance of finding Lucas than any of the experts…but if she happens to stumble onto the people Lucas was running from, I doubt they'd be happy. Does she even own a gun?"

"I doubt it. Somehow I can't see her spending time on a shooting range. But," Zach added, "you never know. Maybe I'd better have a talk with her."

"Can you and your cousins even leave this area once you've started your big twelve-month stay here?"

"For any length of time, no…unless it's a business trip or a short vacation. The will was pretty clear on that score so none of us could maintain our residence elsewhere and just drop into town now and then."

Jack stared down the empty street. "I think she's far less worried about her inheritance than she is about Lucas. But I'm concerned about her surviving a dangerous trip that she's not prepared to take."

"Sounds like you have more than a casual interest in my little cousin."

"We're just neighbors."

"And?"

"Friends."

Zach chuckled. "Tell me another one."

"Whatever I might feel about her, she's definitely not looking for any ties to this area. She has made it clear that she plans to leave for the West Coast, and my career is here. End of story."

"If you say so. Personally, I recently discovered that some things are worth fighting for…and the rewards can far outweigh the costs."

Jack exhaled sharply. "Not when it means taking away someone's dream. From what I hear, she was doing what she loved in San Francisco and left it only to make sure all of you earned your legacy. I think she's already counting the days until she can go back there."

"Well, whatever anyone else might say, I just want you to know that I think you're a great guy…and I've never harbored ill will toward you or your brother. In my book, the people in this town just need to grow up and get along. Period."

"I agree." Jack debated for a moment. "I haven't said anything to anyone else about this, but the other reason I called you was to let you know that I'm heading down to Florida tomorrow."

"You don't need to get involved in Lucas's situation."

"Yes, I do. I spent a semester in that area, studying the environmental impact of the sugar mill industry on the Everglades, so at least some of the area is familiar ground. I've had a lot of experience with search and rescue up here, so that set of skills might help me find Lucas." A note of urgency filled his voice. "I just want to find Lucas myself before Mei goes off on some crazy trip that could get her killed."

"I don't think you should do this."

"You can't go, Zach. You're in law enforcement, and that's outside your jurisdiction. Me? I have no connections, and I don't have to worry about stepping on any toes. I'm the only one of us who could go and not risk real trouble with my career. Besides all that, you might be needed here at that Thanksgiving dinner in a professional capacity."

"How come?"

"Because I issued quite a challenge to Charley and the rest of Samuel's clan, implying that they were too spineless to show up and behave." Jack gave a humorless laugh.

"That just might make them show up and help fulfill Jasmine's dream, but there's *no* way I guarantee that they'll behave."

Mei stepped into the old town hall building on Wednesday afternoon after school and headed for the kitchen in back.

With its old wooden floors, pressed-tin ceiling and dark woodwork, the building harkened to the Old West years. She could imagine it as the General Store it had once been, with ladies in long dresses looking at rolls of pretty sprigged muslin and cowboys loading up on supplies, spurs jangling at their boot heels.

It was hardly like that now. All of the town offices were now housed in a boring, modern one-story building a few blocks away, so this building was just a barren shell rented out for various events. Someone had already set up ten or twelve banquet tables and the chairs, with a long row of tables pushed together along one side for a serving line, a bank of eight empty electric roasters positioned and ready for the meal to come.

In the kitchen, Jasmine pointed to a door by the large sinks with a stalk of celery in her hand. "If that pan needs refrigeration, there's plenty of room in the walk-in."

"It's just a double batch of lemon bars for everyone to enjoy while they decorate and work on Thanksgiving dinner for tomorrow. I felt guilty just ordering pies from Arabella and having them delivered," Mei said.

Jasmine grinned. "Never apologize for calling on her. You know her pastries and pies will be the hit of the whole Thanksgiving dinner."

"If I didn't say it before, I just want to tell you that I am really happy that you decided to host this dinner. I think it will be a turning point for a lot of people in this town, and maybe it will even become a tradition." Mei retied her wool scarf and tossed the ends over her shoulders. "If it does, I'll try to come back every year."

Jasmine's mouth dropped open. "Come back? You're *leaving?*"

"I meant after my twelve-month stint is up. I think I'll miss all of you a lot."

"B-but what about Jack? Aren't you guys, like, an item? Everyone thinks so."

Mei felt a stab of pain at her heart, even as she fluttered her hand in a dismissive gesture.

She'd called him once since that awkward scene at his office on Saturday, but he hadn't called back and she hadn't seen him. Only when she realized that it was over had she recognized the truth.

She'd loved Jack McCord in high school, and she'd been falling in love a little deeper every day since she'd come back to Clayton. But he hadn't cared at all. Not even in friendship, apparently, and now her remaining months here were going to seem like years.

A delicate line formed between Jasmine's eyebrows. "Well, then it's awfully nice for him to help out the family anyway. Right? I mean, expensive and everything."

Mei blinked. "I'm not sure what you mean."

"His trip. I thought for sure he told everyone."

"What are you talking about?"

"He said he wanted to help out our family, so he flew to Florida on Saturday afternoon to find Lucas."

Mei felt her heart lurch. A last-minute decision like that meant his plane tickets had probably cost a fortune. But far worse was the fact that he was placing himself in danger. And for a man who had never even been a close friend. "I…don't understand. Why would he do that, all of a sudden?"

Jasmine rolled her eyes. "Think about it."

Mei stared back at her.

"Haven't you seen the way he looks at you? Duh! When he sat next to you in church it was plain as day." Jasmine laughed. "I think half the church saw it, too, because you both sure received a lot of dirty looks. It reminded me of exactly how it was when Cade and I first started to go together. Like it was going to mean the end of the world or something."

A flicker of hope burst into flame, then quickly died. "I'm sure you're wrong, Jasmine. We're just friends."

"Yeah, right."

"But I still don't get why he would decide to do something like that."

"Zach told Arabella that Jack hoped his search-and-rescue training might help him succeed, even though the other investigators failed. And because Jack isn't a cop, he wouldn't be stepping out of bounds...or something." Jasmine glanced over at the big Clayton Feed Mill calendar on the wall and frowned. "But maybe things aren't going so well for Jack, either. I'm sure Arabella said his return flight was due in this morning, and no one has heard from him."

The cousins all met at the town hall on Thanksgiving morning, bearing dozens of dishes to be stowed away in the walk-in cooler. Jasmine also had the turkeys in there, trussed, stuffed and ready for the oven and her large serving pans of buttery sage dressing and the other dishes she had prepared.

Zach eyed the stack of bakery boxes on a counter by the phone. "I think we need pie."

Jasmine laughed. "We have pie. At least twelve, actually."

"Let me clarify that. I think we ought to *eat* pie because dinner won't be until three o'clock. I'll gladly volunteer one of the pies I brought…er, bought from Arabella. Pecan or bumbleberry?"

"Either." Jasmine held up a hand and began ticking off the items on her fingers. "I do have croissants, several pounds of deli roast beef, ham and chicken, plus swiss lorraine, sharp cheddar and provolone cheeses, so if anyone wants a light lunch, have at it."

Mei halfheartedly listened to the banter, but all she could think about was Jack. She'd already quizzed Zach twice, but there had still been no word from him. If he'd missed his scheduled flight home, wouldn't he have called to let Zach know about that so he wouldn't make a fruitless trip to the airport? Zach had driven forty minutes out of Clayton, only to find that Jack had never gotten on the plane.

Mei had left a text message on Jack's cell phone, but there'd been no answer.

What if he had run into that drug gang? Out in the swamp, bodies would be easy to dispose of—the scent of blood would draw any number of alligators, and remains might never be found.

The weight pressing down on her heart made it hard to breathe as she tried to keep busy hanging orange, gold and brown streamers in swoops across the ceiling. And even the wonderful aromas of roasting turkeys, sweet potatoes and homemade yeast rolls baking in the ovens couldn't take away the fear and worry in her heart.

Please, God, let Jack be okay. I missed my chances before, but just give me one more shot to tell him how much I care.

By three o'clock Jasmine had changed into a pretty bronze silk dress and taken up her station at the front door as hostess, while Mei and her cousins finished loading up the serving tables.

Jasmine opened the door to look outside, then came back in, wringing her hands. "There's no one out there. No one is going to come," she wailed.

Arabella walked over to give her a hug. "You've done a beautiful job, sweetie. Everything is perfect, and no one on our side of the family tree would miss this for the world. If that's the extent of it, you've still made this a great success and we'll just have to enjoy triple helpings. Speaking of that—look."

Jasmine turned to the door, where Jonathan was visible through the front window and on the verge of herding the triplets inside. Behind him there was a growing line of adults. "Thank goodness!"

Mei shooed Arabella away from going back into the kitchen. "I'll take care of replenishing all of this. You go out and be with your family."

"You should be able to do that, too," Arabella protested.

Mei smiled. "I just have my mom in town, and we all know how much she'd like a crowd like this—especially if all the 'wrong' people come. I'll be glad just to keep busy."

Arabella's face fell. "I'm so sorry, Mei. I know how you've worried about your brother. And…well, Jasmine told me she talked to you yesterday. I'm so sorry if things didn't work out with Jack. Honestly, the more I think about it, the more I think you two seem like such a perfect match."

Feeling the warmth of a blush start moving up her cheeks, Mei busied herself with taking a batch of dinner rolls out of the oven, not wanting to see the sympathy in Arabella's eyes. "It was never that way at all. Jasmine is just a bit of a romantic is all."

"She is that," Arabella said with an affectionate laugh. "I just hope Jack makes it home from Florida all right. It was wonderful of him to try to find my brother, but I don't want to think about him risking his life. I've been praying for them both since I heard that Jack left." She waved her hands. "Really, you go on out there—be with your family."

Arabella gave her a quick hug, then went out to meet the triplets who were now running through the front door.

Mei lingered at the door of the kitchen, watching all of the family members pour in—many whom she didn't recognize, though she could see Jasmine at the door, welcoming them all with a hug and clearly charming the socks off of everyone before checking them off her list.

Great-uncle Samuel loomed in the doorway, his features cast in his usual scowl. He hesitated, rolling the brim of his Western hat in his hands as he surveyed the crowd going through the serving line.

Mei held her breath.

Then Jasmine sashayed up to him, gave him a hug and chatted with him for a moment before waving him toward the food with a smile. He moved on and Vincent followed, his eyes downcast and the tips of his ears bright red. Then over a dozen strangers followed—men, women and children—but Jasmine merrily marked them off her list as they walked in, so they must be part of Samuel's extended family.

The group moved as one toward the tables in the back corner, barely glancing at anyone they passed through the growing crowd. They all marked off their separate territories by draping their coats on the chairs. They were as far away as possible from the George Sr. side of the family and none of them looked happy but, incredibly, they were *here*.

"Good for you, Jasmine," Mei said under her breath as she went back into the kitchen for another pan of mashed potatoes. "You're half the age of most people here, and you accomplished something no one else could."

The tables were nearly full now, and still more people were coming.

Reverend West walked in and gave Jasmine a quick hug, then called for a table prayer. When everyone rose, he cleared his throat. "I appreciate the dinner invitation. It's wonderful to see all of you here—a good share of my flock—enjoying fellowship and a celebration of this day." He took a moment to sweep the room with a genial smile. "My hope is that all of you will continue these gatherings in years to come, in a spirit of love and harmony, and that the meal we share will be the beginning of greater friend-ships and happiness."

A number of guests shifted uncomfortably, and in the far corner, Samuel grimaced.

Reverend West continued. "And now, Lord, we ask Your blessings upon each and every one of us. We give thanks to You for the bounty we enjoy in our lives each and every day and the bounty we are about to receive. Please bless and keep us in Your grace, now and forever, Amen."

Jasmine moved from one table to the next, dismissing people toward the buffet line. She carefully alternated be-tween the groups from different sides of the family, smil-ing and touching a shoulder here, offering a hug or a kiss on a cheek there.

Mei smiled as she replenished the buffet line and watched Jasmine welcome everyone.

Mei noticed that Cade lingered at his father's table for a while, one hand on the back of Charley's chair, and ap-peared to be talking earnestly to him. A few minutes later he walked away, shaking his head in apparent disgust, and disappeared out a side door.

Concerned, Mei followed and stepped out into the chilly breeze. She found him leaning against the side of the building, his head bowed.

"Are you all right?" she ventured. "It's kind of cold to be out here without a coat."

He looked up sharply, the flash of irritation in his eyes fading as he saw who she was. "I keep trying to do the right thing. And it just never works out."

"What happened?"

"Jack keeps telling me how he regrets that he never had a relationship with his real dad. And of course Charley was no substitute."

"I think every guy—no matter how old he is—wants a good relationship with his father."

Cade kicked at a clump of snow. "Ever since I got engaged, Dad has been really ticked off at me. Jack says I should try harder to reconcile with him before the wedding so there aren't hard feelings. He says I'll always regret it if Dad won't come to the ceremony."

"Jack is a wise man."

"Maybe he's got the right idea, but he ought to know better. My dad is stubborn as an ole mule and twice as cranky." Cade looked over his shoulder and lowered his voice even though no one else was around. "You want to know what he and Pauley were talking about when I went over to try one more time?"

"Would I be right in guessing it wasn't about the turkey?"

Cade slashed the air with the side of his hand. "They were talking about how coming to Jasmine's dinner was just a chance for a little reconnaissance. Like it was an army mission or something to come here and spy on the enemy."

"Maybe they were joking?"

"You didn't hear them. Jasmine put on this dinner out of the goodness of her heart, and all they can think of is finding ways to tear down everything good that she's tried to do." He clenched his jaw. "It makes me so angry. Pauley even said something about me not having a clue about the true depth of what's going on—as if they're all cooking up something really bad."

"Maybe that's all hot air. This dinner is a wonderful start, even if change can't happen overnight. I'll bet this day will help spur gradual changes that will make a great difference down the road."

"I hope so." Cade shivered and rubbed his arms.

"I *know* so."

"I came out here to cool off, and I guess I'm now just about frozen," he said ruefully. "I guess we oughta get back inside. Thanks, Mei."

Most of the crowd had gone back for seconds and thirds when one more lone, slender figure appeared at the door. *Mom?*

Mei set aside her pot holders and flew to the front door. "You came!"

"I had to, dear. It seems everyone else in town is right here, and there was no point in roasting a turkey at home. Will you sit with me?"

Mei hugged her, then led the way to the serving line. "I haven't eaten yet, so I would love that."

They found empty places at a front table vacated by a pair of guests who'd had to get back to their ranch.

"You ended up with quite a crowd." Lisette slowly scanned the tables, her mouth forming a moue of distaste when her gaze skimmed past the Samuel Clayton family. "I'm surprised they came."

"I'm glad they did. It's time we all erased the bitterness and tried to start anew. I think Jasmine's dinner has been a great start, don't you?"

Lisette cut a small bite of turkey. "Maybe. But it's far more than mere pettiness that caused all the trouble in the past. And you'd do well to remember it."

"You know, we all make out Samuel's clan as the bad guys, but it didn't start out that way. If George Sr. hadn't cheated Samuel out of his fair share of the family's money and land, maybe they would have gotten along as loving brothers, not enemies."

"You hardly need to tell me that, dear." Lisette sniffed.

"I mean, I don't condone any wrong that might have been done, but I can understand why there's been some deep resentment against us over the years."

"I'd rather not discuss it." Lisette glanced around the room. "I don't see that friend of yours here."

Something in her tone—a hint of smugness—made Mei flinch. "He's not."

"Well, that's a relief. I think Jack was a bit of a social climber, don't you? Perhaps he learned his place."

Embarrassment rushed through Mei as she studied her mother's placid, satisfied expression. "What did you do, Mom? Did you say something to him?"

The almost imperceptible shrug of her shoulder said it all.

"Oh, *Mom.*" After their long discussion over the weekend, Mei had imagined that she and her mother had reached a deeper level of understanding. But nothing had changed after all. "Why did you have to do something like that?"

"It was for your own good."

Mei bit back a cry of disbelief. "If you think he's not good enough, you couldn't be more wrong."

"You have no idea how wrong *you* are, Mei." Lisette leaned forward. "We had to do it once before, you know. Your dad and I, back when you were in high school. Your father heard through the family grapevine that Jack was developing an impossible crush on you, and we had to nip *that* problem in the bud. I just had another talk with him is all. He understood. He's a bright enough boy to see the truth."

Mei's dinner turned to dust in her stomach. "I don't know if I can ever forgive you for this. I'll try because I know in some strange way you think you are protecting me. But you are so wrong about him."

"When you're a little older you'll—"

"Understand? No, I won't. I'll always regret that I lost a chance with Jack. Always." She released a long, frustrated breath. "Do you know what he's doing right now? He flew to Florida. He went to search for Lucas, Mom. He figured that his search-and-rescue training would help him succeed even when the law enforcement officers down there failed. He wanted to bring Lucas back to us."

Lisette paled.

"Jasmine told me he left Saturday and was due back Tuesday, but he didn't come back on his flight. No one has heard from him since. The man who you think isn't worthy of me may have lost his life trying to save your son."

Lisette looked over Mei's shoulder, her eyes widening. "Mei."

"I'm sorry." Mei took a steadying breath to rein in her emotions. "I guess I'm a little upset about this."

"Apparently. But you shouldn't be. I'm back…and I'm not going anywhere."

She froze at the sound of the familiar, deep voice, dimly

aware of the sudden silence in the room. Her heart hammered against her ribs as she rose to her feet and slowly turned around.

Jack stood behind her, a jagged gash that should've had stitches trailing across one cheek, a dark bruise on the other. He still had the strap of a duffel bag slung over his shoulder.

He looked so weary, so incredibly wonderful, that she impulsively threw her arms around him. "Where have you been? What happened?"

He winced, then dropped his bag to the floor and gingerly wrapped his arms around her. He brushed a kiss on her forehead. Then reached up and tucked her head beneath his chin. "Maybe don't hold on *quite* so tight. I'm a little bit banged up. But the good news is that I did find Lucas. The drug dealers are in jail, that little boy's safe and Lucas will be coming home."

They were suddenly surrounded by the family—Brooke and Arabella and Zach, and then all the others who were shouting out questions and laughing and crying.

And then Lisette was there, too, working her way through the crowd.

"You found my son?" she whispered, her voice trembling. "He's coming home—and he's all right?"

Jack must have overheard every one of her arrogant words as he was coming into the hall, but he smiled at her without any sign of rancor. "Yes, ma'am. Hopefully he'll be home in a few days, and he's looking forward to seeing you very much."

Lisette's soft smile flickered. "I think you're being generous with me. My good Lord knows Lucas and I didn't always get along. But maybe now I'll have a chance to do things right. Thank you."

Arabella, bless her heart, shouted, "Time for pie!"

The crowd turned away to form a line at the dessert table, leaving Jack, Lisette and Mei alone.

"I went after Lucas because of your daughter, Lisette." Jack lowered his voice. "When you told me she planned to leave town at the end of her year here and wanted no attachments holding her back, I figured finding her brother was one last gift I could give her. But while I was gone, I realized something else. This isn't the time or the place, but after this day is over, Mei and I need to talk."

By the time the dinner was over and all of the mess was cleaned up, it was nearly eight o'clock at night. Before he'd even eaten half his dinner Jack had been called away on a search-and-rescue mission involving a missing girl at the far end of the county, and Mei hadn't heard from him since.

Now, on Friday morning, Mei had picked up Macy for a scheduled outing and the two of them had gone to Erin's acreage to look at all of the animals. Mei and Erin stood at either side of a blue roan mare's halter, while Macy sat on top. "Do you like horses, Macy?"

The child looked down at Mei and tried to smile. The morning caregiver had drawn Mei aside to let her know that Darlene had had a rough night and wasn't doing well at all. As much as everyone tried to shield Macy from the truth, she clearly understood that her mother's days were numbered.

Macy petted the horse's heavy winter coat. "How come she's so thin?"

"This is a rescue horse, honey," Erin explained. "She was in a place where the owners didn't care for her properly, so I've been feeding her really well."

Macy frowned. "Why wouldn't someone take care of such a pretty horse?"

"Some people run out of money. Sometimes they don't know any better. And sometimes they're just careless or thoughtless or mean and don't remember that their pets are God's creatures, too. If we have pets, we need to love and care for them every single day."

Macy nodded somberly. "Like all the ladies who come to take care of my mama?"

Erin shot a quick, pained glance at Mei. "Sort of like that, sweetie. Of course, your mom is even more important."

"I'd like to take care of people or animals when I grow up. I could be a nurse or a doctor or a vet'narian."

Her heart breaking for this poor child, Mei fixed a bright smile on her face. "My brother, Lucas, went to school to be a vet, so he takes care of animals every day. When he comes back here, maybe you can visit his clinic someday. He'll be back any day now."

Erin paled. "Really? I thought he was…"

Mei nodded. "Jack McCord went to Florida after him. I haven't heard all the details yet, but at our Thanksgiving dinner yesterday, Jack announced that Lucas was on his way home."

"That's…wonderful." Erin swallowed hard. "You and your mom must be thrilled."

Curious, Mei looked over the mare's neck at her. "Were you and Lucas friends?"

"Barely. Small-town school, you know—everyone knows just about everyone else, at least a little. I remember him being a…a nice kid." Erin patted Macy's leg and smiled up at her. "Okay, Miss Macy—are you ready for us to go at a walk with you on board?"

At midnight Moose barked softly and lumbered to his feet from where he lay on the floor next to Mei's bed. He poked her temple with his cold, damp nose. Waited. Then poked at her ear before barking again.

Mei awoke with a start and sat bolt upright in bed.

The barks and the sound of soft knocking at the door had seemed part of a dream, but now, blinking away her momentary confusion, she heard another quiet knock and detected Jack's voice. Moose galloped to the door and barked again, his tail waving madly.

"Mei? It's just me—Jack."

She'd gone to bed wearing sweatpants and a sweatshirt, and now she scuffed on her slippers and grabbed a robe on her way to the door. After checking through the peephole in the door, she unlocked it and found Jack on the porch. From his weary eyes to the slump of his shoulders and dirt-smudged face, he looked exhausted.

"I just got back to town," he said. "Sorry to wake you up, but I just couldn't wait."

The turbulent emotions playing across his face sent a spear of worry through her. "Did you find that little girl? Was she all right?"

"We had volunteers from two counties and two search dogs out there looking for her. We found her two miles from home just over an hour ago. Mild frostbite and other exposure issues, but she'll be okay."

Moose pressed against her leg, his entire body vibrating with excitement at seeing a friend. She urged him through the door and the dog licked Jack's hand, then bounded outside to do his business. Wrapping her arms around her waist, she stepped out onto the porch to try to keep an eye on him. "I'm so glad to see you back safe and sound."

"Yeah, well…" His voice trailed off and he looked down at her. "It's what we do."

"You must be frozen to the bone. Can I make you some coffee? Hot chocolate?"

"I'd better head for home. I just wanted to stop in and say what I had no time to say at the dinner."

She felt a shiver run through her that had nothing to do with the cold night air.

"In the past week, your mom, Charley and his cronies have let me know that this is a bad idea. For different reasons, though—your mom because she loves you, Charley because he is a twisted old man who doesn't really care if I'm happy or not."

Her pulse fluttered. "B-bad idea?"

"But though neither intended it that way, they helped me realize that I couldn't just let you go, no matter who tried to stand in the way. I had to try to make it work this time around."

Speechless, she looked up into his beautiful blue eyes and, despite the cold, felt warmth flow through her when he gently rested his hands on her shoulders.

"Your mom says you can't wait to go back to your job in San Francisco. I know you've said it also, but my career is here…so maybe I shouldn't stand in your way when it comes to a job that makes you truly happy."

She struggled to find her voice. "There are a lot of jobs that can make me happy, Jack. Finding the right person to spend a life with is much, much harder."

"I can't argue with you there." He swallowed hard. "And the truth is…I can't just walk away without trying harder to find out if things could ever work out between us. I love you, Mei. I think I did way back in high school, though I was too young to even see it."

"Me, too," she whispered.

Moose bounded up the steps and skidded across the porch, all awkward legs and madly wagging tail, as if he knew this moment meant something good about his favorite humans. His furry body knocked Mei into Jack's arms, then he shook off a shower of snow that filled the air with weightless diamonds.

Jack gently brushed some snowflakes from Mei's nose. The laughter and love in his eyes matched her feelings exactly as he lowered her mouth to hers for a sweet kiss. "I think your dog likes me well enough, but now I just have to hope that you do, too."

Her heart overflowing, Mei reached up and pulled him down for a longer, even sweeter kiss that sent tingles clear to her toes. "That's a question you don't even have to ask."

* * * * *

Dear Reader,

I hope you have been enjoying each month of the six-book Love Inspired Rocky Mountain Heirs series, which began in July and will end in December 2011. Five of my favorite authors are a part of this series, and they were all absolutely wonderful to work with!

The Loner's Thanksgiving Wish is a story that spoke to my heart. It deals with the problems of fitting in and of being different, and the fresh perspective one can have if they return home later, a little older and wiser. It also is the story of two people who were deeply attracted to one another back in high school but who never would have had a chance to be together back then, given their family circumstances. How many of us have wondered about the special gal or guy we knew when we were young?

I love to hear from readers! You can contact me by snail mail at P.O. Box 2550, Cedar Rapids, IA, 52406; through my website at www.roxannerustand.com; or at my blog (the All Creatures Great and Small place) at http://roxannerustand.blogspot.com.

Take care, and God bless!

Roxanne

Questions for Discussion

1. Mei's late grandfather added stipulations to his will that required each of the six cousins to spend an entire year back in their hometown. Why do you think he made this effort to control their actions from the grave? Do you think it was fair, or should he have simply left orders to distribute his estate?

2. The two factions of the Clayton family have been feuding for years, going back to some nefarious doings on the part of George Sr. Have you had to deal with difficult family situations like this? How could this have been resolved long ago?

3. Despite her legal adoption, Mei never felt she was a real part of her extended family, or a part of the town. Her feelings were reinforced by her grandfather, who clearly treated her like an outsider. Were you adopted, or have there been adoptions in your family? How do you think the risk of such feelings of alienation could be avoided?

4. At one point, Lisette is surprised to hear that Mei never felt close to her when growing up. Now that Mei is grown, do you think those wounds can ever be healed? Or would that damage run too deep? Do you have unresolved issues with your own mother or daughter?

5. Darlene Perry still refuses to identify Macy's father, and as she is on her deathbed, that secret could die with her. What do you think about a father's rights

when an illegitimate child is involved? Is it ever best to just keep those secrets, or does a child always have a right to know?

6. Who do you think is Macy's real father?

7. Jasmine and Cade are just eighteen and plan to get married no matter what anyone thinks. What do you think about such a young marriage? Can it work? What are the pros and cons? What would you do about this, if Jasmine was your own daughter?

8. Mei had strong feelings for Jack back in high school, and now believes her feelings never really died. Do you know high school sweethearts who parted and met years later? Do you think such a "once-in-a-lifetime love" is just a fantasy, a grasp at one's youth, or that it can be something real?

9. Lisette has a hardened heart toward the other side of the family, in part because of the terrible rumors they started about her son, Lucas. What do you think about the possibility of forgiveness and moving on in a situation like this? Is Lisette wise to still keep her distance and be wary of everyone who was involved?

10. Lucas grew up behaving like a rebel, and there is still friction between him and his mother. Do you think this stems directly from Lisette's behavior toward him over the years he grew up, or do you think this would have been Lucas's personality no matter what?

11. Jack has come to town to try to be a good influence for Cade, since Cade's father was lackadaisical. Do

you think siblings can nurture each other well enough to mediate the damage a poor parent can inflict?

12. Jasmine thinks she can change the entire negative family dynamic by hosting a big family dinner and forcing everyone to "play nice." In real life, do you think this would work? If you have strife in your own family, what positive steps could you take to improve those relationships? What efforts have succeeded—or failed—in the past?

13. Mei followed her heart into teaching, and her brother became a vet instead of going into medicine. Both careers were an apparent disappointment to their parents, who had held both of their children up to high ideals and had rigid notions about what their children should become. How much influence should a parent have on their child's future? Did your own parents express strong opinions about your future? What about your feelings about your own children?

14. The community church members have taken Darlene Perry and her daughter under their wing, and spend many volunteer hours helping her cope with her terminal illness. What volunteer opportunities exist in your own church and community? What have you done to make your community a better place? Do you feel you made a difference?

15. Initially, Mei feels that God hasn't really been in her corner all these years—that He doesn't listen to her prayers. But He does—in His own perfect way, and in His own perfect timing. Discuss how some

of your own prayers have been answered. Were the answers what you expected? Did they come as soon as you'd hoped?

INSPIRATIONAL

Wholesome romances that touch the heart and soul.

Love Inspired

COMING NEXT MONTH
AVAILABLE NOVEMBER 22, 2011

THE CHRISTMAS QUILT
Brides of Amish Country
Patricia Davids

THE PRODIGAL'S CHRISTMAS REUNION
Rocky Mountain Heirs
Kathryn Springer

HIS HOLIDAY FAMILY
A Town Called Hope
Margaret Daley

THE COWBOY'S HOLIDAY BLESSING
Cooper Creek
Brenda Minton

YULETIDE HEARTS
Men of Allegany County
Ruth Logan Herne

MISTLETOE MATCHMAKER
Moonlight Cove
Lissa Manley

REQUEST YOUR FREE BOOKS!

2 FREE INSPIRATIONAL NOVELS
PLUS 2
FREE
MYSTERY GIFTS

YES! Please send me 2 FREE Love Inspired® novels and my 2 FREE mystery gifts (gifts are worth about $10). After receiving them, if I don't wish to receive any more books, I can return the shipping statement marked "cancel." If I don't cancel, I will receive 6 brand-new novels every month and be billed just $4.49 per book in the U.S. or $4.99 per book in Canada. That's a saving of at least 22% off the cover price. It's quite a bargain! Shipping and handling is just 50¢ per book in the U.S. and 75¢ per book in Canada.* I understand that accepting the 2 free books and gifts places me under no obligation to buy anything. I can always return a shipment and cancel at any time. Even if I never buy another book, the two free books and gifts are mine to keep forever.

105/305 IDN FEGR

Name _____ (PLEASE PRINT) _____

Address _____ Apt. # _____

City _____ State/Prov. _____ Zip/Postal Code _____

Signature (if under 18, a parent or guardian must sign)

Mail to the **Reader Service:**
IN U.S.A.: P.O. Box 1867, Buffalo, NY 14240-1867
IN CANADA: P.O. Box 609, Fort Erie, Ontario L2A 5X3

Not valid for current subscribers to Love Inspired books.

**Are you a subscriber to Love Inspired books
and want to receive the larger-print edition?
Call 1-800-873-8635 or visit www.ReaderService.com.**

* Terms and prices subject to change without notice. Prices do not include applicable taxes. Sales tax applicable in N.Y. Canadian residents will be charged applicable taxes. Offer not valid in Quebec. This offer is limited to one order per household. All orders subject to credit approval. Credit or debit balances in a customer's account(s) may be offset by any other outstanding balance owed by or to the customer. Please allow 4 to 6 weeks for delivery. Offer available while quantities last.

Your Privacy—The Reader Service is committed to protecting your privacy. Our Privacy Policy is available online at www.ReaderService.com or upon request from the Reader Service.

We make a portion of our mailing list available to reputable third parties that offer products we believe may interest you. If you prefer that we not exchange your name with third parties, or if you wish to clarify or modify your communication preferences, please visit us at www.ReaderService.com/consumerschoice or write to us at Reader Service Preference Service, P.O. Box 9062, Buffalo, NY 14269. Include your complete name and address.

LIREG11B

When former Amishman Gideon Troyer sees his Amish ex-girlfriend on television at a quilt auction to raise money for surgery to correct her blindness, he's stunned and feels a pull drawing him back to his past.

Read on for a sneak preview of
THE CHRISTMAS QUILT
by Patricia Davids.

Rebecca Beachy pulled the collar of her coat closed against a cold gust of wind and ugly memories. An early storm was on its way, but God had seen fit to hold it off until the quilt auction was over. For that, she was thankful.

When she and her aunt finally reached their seats, Rebecca unbuttoned her coat and removed her heavy bonnet. Many of the people around her greeted her in her native Pennsylvania Dutch. Leaning closer to her aunt, she asked, "Is my *kapp* on straight? Do I look okay?"

"And why wouldn't you look okay?" Vera asked.

"Because I may have egg yolk from breakfast on my dress, or my back may be covered with dust from the buggy seat. I don't know. Just tell me I look presentable." She knew everyone would be staring at her when her quilt was brought up for auction. She didn't like being the center of attention.

"You look lovely." The harsh whisper startled her.

She turned her face toward the sound coming from behind her and caught the scent of a man's spicy aftershave. The voice must belong to an *Englisch* fellow. *"Danki."*

"You're most welcome." He coughed, and she realized he was sick.

"You sound as if you should be abed with that cold."

"So I've been told," he admitted.

"It is a foolish fellow who doesn't follow *goot* advice.

"Some people definitely consider me foolish." His raspy voice held a hint of amusement.

He was poking fun at himself. She liked that. There was something familiar about him, but she couldn't put her finger on what it was. "Have we met?"

To see if Rebecca and Gideon can let go of the past
and move forward to a future together, pick up
THE CHRISTMAS QUILT by Patricia Davids
Available in December
from Love Inspired Books.

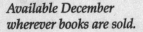